Reptilian Wolf

|I|

A Folie in New York

By the Werths
Xherdan Werth

From Hurry to the Capsule Atelier

ISBN : 978-1-7774959-4-7 Paperback

ISBN : 978-1-7774959-5-4 Ebook

A Hurry to the Capsule book

v 1.0

Diorama by Katherine Conrad

Photo by Spider Palace

Cover design by YoubO

Also by the Werths

Currently Available on ebook and paperback

The Apprentice's Butler
I. To Be Prince On Maui
II. In the Middle Lies the River
III. You Drown In Your Own Water

Stillborn Ecdysis
I. Came the Hoopoe
II. Flew the Bird's Hunter: Episode Yemen

Reptilian Wolf
I. A Folie in New York
II. The Estuary in Boston (soon)

"Read First, Buy Later"

The following work is distributed on a "read first, buy later" principle.

You have the possibility of getting this book for free, or copying/borrowing the book of a friend with the blessing of the collective for your first read.

If you read it and found something in this book, please consider supporting it on the internet or sharing it with your entourage. Do not underestimate the impact of an insightful comment, whether positive or negative, and a cheer or a share; they go a long way.

If you can afford financial support and think this book and the Werths writings are worth an investment, please consider buying the book.

For more information, please check Hurry to the Capsule website.

We appreciate your patronage in any capacity; it allows us to bring more books to the public and elevate the quality of our work.

Forward

We buy time here
so we can fuck each other.
Everyone hasn't gone to the moon. Some of us are still
here,
breathing heavy,
navigating this deadly
sexual turbulence;
perhaps we are the unlucky ones
At the end of heavy breathing
who will be responsible
for the destruction of human love?
Who are the heartless sons of bitches
sucking blood from dreams
as they are born?
Who has the guts
to come forward
and testify?

Essex Hemphill – Heavy Breathing

Tip your bartenders.
Some are Gods in human flesh.
Few provide the communal spirit for the broken and
wounded.
Rare ones are cradles of humanity
To Paul R. K.,
Who miraculously still likes people, despite relentlessly
dealing with them
Who has an eye for the soul in them, despite the abyssal
tar they so often bathe in
And, who in his humbling wisdom, often says "I don't
know" and "I don't understand" and "Back then, I didn't
understand"
I love you

To the Love Alcove

I assess the lonely figure hunched over the bar as I pack my synthesizer; everything about him is stillness, save for the hands furiously scribbling. For some messed up reason, I think of my mother. While the rest of my band, the Syntho-usikeers, is wrapping up and getting ready to leave, I contemplate whether I should grab a drink or call it a night. It has been a slow day at the Greenwich Village studio, and tomorrow will be another shift at the tacky lobby hotel. I knew what grabbing a drink would entail; am I in the mood for a hunt? How far will I theoretically take it? Can I afford the realistic outcome of the night?

"Hey! Are you coming?"

"Go ahead."

I head to the bar and order a beer. I openly push next to the lonely man; he has about my height and a fuller figure. He is furtive and awkward. Despite the bearded face, his lines betray the old teenager, the hesitant adult. He steals a glance at me, then hastily gathers whatever he had in his hands to his chest. He puts his palm on his cheek, and contemplates my face and my torso; he is tipsy, has deer eyes and a shy smile. I can easily make up a foreignness about him, and the awkward demeanor of a self-conscious outsider. There is also something stuttering about his manners that I have learned to identify. All my observations lead me to a final assessment: He has all that I find to be serious coinage. I greet him with my pleasant and safe tone:

"Good evening stranger."

He giggles and mutters a simple 'good evening' back. He is quiet afterwards, and doesn't know where to look. Serious coinage indeed.

"What brings you here? ... From the other side of the ocean? ... Tourism?"

Tourists have increasingly swarmed the streets of New York. Few years ago, to find them beyond the City, in niche and intimate portions, was uncommon. But these are the '90s and there is nothing sacred enough anymore about the parochial neighborhoods within every decent borough. By some magical tour de force, New York stopped belonging to New Yorkers, and was the property of labels and tourists.

"Where are you from?"

He giggles and shrugs.

"Here and there ... why?"

I sense a defensiveness. This one's instinct may be right, but there is nothing to fear, not on that end at least. Besides, he is in New York, not some lost Bible Belt hole.

And I happen to like the foreignness in him. If it's the correct row in that library, I am game, and so he is.

"You don't look like the typical New Yorker of the underground techno pop scene."

He attempts a scoff and says:

"Neither do you."

It's true; my neat clothes and studied manners don't read electronic new wave musician. Yet, as I heard Lady Mama once say, I don't know of anyone from my generation who poured the epiphanies of their age and the salt of their sweat in a Moog the way I did. This might not be as impressive as it sounds though. The poster children of 70s and 80s futuristic music are aesthetically driven contrarians, and youngsters on high highs and low lows. No one takes them seriously to commission them, save for videogames or campy soundtracks. I doubt they take themselves seriously in matters of artistic creation anyway. It's the most problematic feature of the branch of music where my artistic proclivity thrives. Therefore, no one expects excellence or chases expertise in the craft. And no one expects the well-spoken, tie-wearing bald man to be an electronic new wave musician, even less one who knows enough of the instruments down to their hardware and algorithms.

Going back to the stranger, I wonder whether he does not want to acknowledge his foreignness. There must be something about where he is coming from then, and that could be serious coinage. There would be something deeply hidden, dismissive and embarrassing about his inclinations. It would be the affair of a night. I would get my fill, and we could both disappear into the light of dawn. With some luck, he would be a virgin too. A powerful asset in these uncertain times, when two thirds of Chelsea do not want to get tested, and the rest are either exhausted partners, absolute dicks or old conquests. Perhaps he had clumsily played before, and is still a virgin in his head. Perhaps he is exercising his own cautious flirt. I assess him and know enough that he is not playing dumb; that at least is out of the way. I need him to speak more.

"So... You're here for someone... In particular?"

"Not really."

He doesn't give me much to work with. Serious coinage. I state.

"I'm Josef."

He extends his hand. I find the gesture funny and I add with a smile.

"And I don't shake hands."

"Ah sorry. Nice to meet you, Josef."

"You?"

"I'm Mo."

"Nice to meet you Mo, from here and there."

We both chuckle while he recovers from what he deems an embarrassing episode. Refusing to shake a stranger's hand shouldn't be so. And yet, it takes him few moments to trust the conversation's flow again, and grant me some attention. I take the opportunity, and glance at his hands; they are strong, with long fingers, bumps on dominating ones. They are hairy in a soft manner, evenly brown and don't look bony and veiny at all. They are absolutely lovely. What a prize.

"Snobbish question Mo; what is it like to be from here AND there?"

He shrugs. Oh, how he pleases me at every turn.

"I don't know. It's its own thing, much like that music you guys were playing."

"Oh, you paid attention to the concert?"

"A little... Enough to know it's not of my taste. I mean no disrespect. But, I came down here thinking there would be some sort of jazz. And this is nothing... Absolutely nothing like jazz."

I barely wince while scoffing. I'm getting much better at redirecting that reflex at this point.

"Jazz in New York... How predictable indeed. No wonder you'd assume that. They got you good, though."

Mo giggles and shrugs. His manners definitely read late adolescence. His stares are stealthy. I can't decide whether by this point, I know his face to like it enough. But what does it matter: By the look of it and with some well-played movements, that face will be buried in a pillow laboring to breathe. I smile from the loveliness of the vision. He shyly smiles back and says.

"You got me good to be honest."

"How so?"

There is a faint accent in his words, but his measured speech is controlled enough that he doesn't let it out. Is that much control necessary? Maybe... If he deals with many nosy ones like me, that is. He must have had some initial contact, most likely unsuccessful. Or maybe he chickened out at some point.

"I saw the sort of audience here and thought they didn't look like jazz listeners. But then, you walked on stage, all sophisticated, with that fancy piano, and I assumed it's some genre of NYC jazz that I have never heard before."

For a shy person, Mo is genuine when he manages to speak beyond few words. I can work with that.

"Being sophisticated is the least you could demonstrate in the Big Apple. Otherwise, it's just an embarrassment to pretend you belong here."

"Pretend... You don't belong here?"

"No one really belongs to New York, at least for a generation and some by now... To start with, this city was nothing but an idea. And this idea no longer applies to this place."

Mo is openly fascinated with my speech. Or maybe these gorgeous big eyes of his magnify otherwise flat feelings.

"Let me order you something that pretends to be real and New Yorker... Two dry Rob Roys. No skewers."

I get us two glasses, and he smiles while trying the drink.

"Ouf... This tastes too strong."

"It's adequate for the winter weather. Take your time. You don't have to sip it at once."

He nods and tries again.

"Why wouldn't you shake my hand?"

The question is abrupt. I'm used to such scenarios, though. I smile and ask:

"Why would I shake your hand?"

"Isn't it the polite thing to do?"

"Maybe 'there'... But here, people don't touch strangers, and have no time for polite gestures."

"Believe it or not, I figured this out by myself. But I thought, since you initiated the conversation..."

"It doesn't mean I would shake your hand. Anymore handshake-related questions?"

He downs his drink and shakes his head. I scoff then ask:

"You're here for college?"

He giggles and replies back, with a semblance of outrage:

"Do I look like such a dorky herb?"

"You read 'virgin' in all manners, unlike someone who excels at being a New Yorker. Yet, you are clearly beyond survival mode, unlike much of those who have been making a living here. What does that leave? Not many options. It may be a big city for all sorts of folks; at least that was the idea... But most people are more or less the same. Add money to the mix, and you can discern who's who."

He nods, impressed. What a gullible youngster, and what a fine night it is turning out to be. I could drift in a state of anticipation, and orient the conversation towards more sensual grounds. But I want to stay in the moment, and enjoy the wide eyes and their fascination.

He tentatively asks:

"I don't want to sound rude, but how old are you?"

"As in normal years.... Or something else?"

"It's just that... I don't see many people my age with bald heads like that."

"Hah! You don't fancy bald guys?"

I pass my hand on the bald head. I feel the hair already poking, and I make a mental note of shaving tonight before anything else. I wouldn't want such a hand running on a spiky patch of skin. For a moment, I summon the image of the bathroom by the Love Alcove: I'm certain there is a razor there, as well as a bar of soap and some handy kits for getting down.

"I don't mind. I mean..."

"Good then. I'm old enough to understand you are more clueless than me, but young enough to be in the same boat as you."

From the way Mo nervously ruffles his dark hair, I am guessing he is worried about his own scalp. I find the insecurity laughable. If this is what younger folks are afraid of these days, I am more than well set. I focus again on his hands; they are soft-looking and removed from any sort of hard labor.

The hint of the forearms is enough in my books to get me there.

I want to know what he does for education, get him to speak more. Most likely a university rat. They would not shut up about university's life, or its lack thereof. I know that. I have been a university rat. Wherever I go, I can recognize my old specie. Most carry on being rats, or at least some breed of rodents. With time, being ill-equipped to a place other than controlled environments of a particular brand of filth makes them idiotic preys. In addition, being more inclined to building shaky convictions from books rather than living life themselves cements the vice of cowardice. They even turn it into virtue in their heads. I am aware I have some distaste for them, but I can't deny how easier my night rounds are thanks to their paper convictions.

"I came here for university."

"Let me guess; finance?... Then law?... Don't tell me something boring like a doctor or an engineer? No, right? You don't look the type."

Actually, Mo does look the type and it would have been serious coinage. But he keeps shaking his head.

"Don't get my hopes up now... An accountant?"

Mo laughs. The first genuine laugh of the evening. We are getting somewhere after all, though by unrefined means.

"God no... Do accountants even come to underground clubs like these, and have drinks on their own?"

"If you think about it, it would make absolute sense that accountants would come to such places alone, and drink by the front bar, like the true herbs they are."

He thinks about it and shakes his head. He motions to the bartender, but I intervene.

"How about you let Roy settle inside? It's already a tough drink on its own... You don't want to get too drunk and become a bore, now, do you?"

Did he make up his mind already? I didn't.

"I see your point... Josef."

"So?"

"But I'm not an accountant, or here for accounting... I'm... In architecture for an advanced university degree."

"Architecture? In New York? Hm... Curious choice."

The closeted artistic type. I'm not sure I like that. This one may be tricky after all. I don't mind him being in the closet for one thing. Two is a crowd, and when there are two, there is plenty. I remind myself this would be a one-night occasion anyway. There is no harm, there is no danger. Why am I uncertain? I don't like being uncertain like that; my life is riddled with uncertainties as it is. I play with uncertainty in my craft at every note. Therefore, I would like certitude in every other mundane matter, the most obvious being what I am getting into, for a night.

"I know, I know... I just..."

Mo decides not to share his reasons, and is quiet for a moment. He then slides his hand on my lap.

"Tell me... Tell me one thing... I'm sorry if it's offensive, but I want no trouble... Are you okay down there? All good?"

The first movement to play. The perfect question to ask. Serious coinage.

"I'm clean."

I have been looking forward to this part. I just didn't expect him to make the first move. I take his hand and bring it to my groin.

Second movement.

"My pipes are clean. And they are fantastically tuned. Take it from an artistic technician."

Mo nods with shy enthusiasm. I wonder whether I'm dealing with an inexperienced young adult or some idiot who is too embarrassed to act like himself. What does it matter; once the night is spent, he will go his merry way and I will go mine.

"What about you?"

He is hesitant in his 'yes'. I gently press his hand and lower my voice.

"I would prefer a straightforward answer. The night is still young for the both of us after all."

He finally stops escaping my gaze and is troubled. He nods.

"I'm good. Never done the stuff, though. I don't know if I'm even good. Some mind that, that's why I didn't..."

That's more than enough for me to get some answers; his Middle Eastern accent and virginal panic reassure me and increase my delight. There are no risks with such a blank page, and there will be no attachments either. I make my decision right there, and state with a confident smile:

"I know a place. You'd come?"

"I would."

His enthusiasm is awkward; I get the vague feeling it is due to an inner conflict. He's not outside his head right now. Do I ask? Do I care?

"No monkey business, though."

"No."

"Because... Just in case..."

I drag his hand so his head is close to me and mutter:

"I have a razor, and I know how to play it just as well as my 'piano'. So, no monkey business."

And this is the third movement. I give Mo his space, and reluctantly, his hand back. I let him take it in and decide. If he wants out, it will be fine. There would be someone else and this delicious memory. There is no rush. Anticipation is key. It's delight on its own. But should he say yes...

"Then... Should we go... To that place?"

I grab my synthesizer and Mo grabs a notebook by his side. I pay and we leave. He follows me without questions. When we get in the cab and I give the address, he doesn't know the place, but doesn't ask. We sit in silence, the instrument between us, as he stares through the window at the buildings. We are out of the glaucous scene of the bar and into the cold night. It is snowing in New York, yet there is still motion in the streets of midtown. Soon, we get to the desolate side of the meatpacking district. I make room within my head for the lovely night ahead, make a space where nothing of the real world and my daylight life would transpire. Let Mo be far away from it, and let me be far away from his own mayhem. He may seem the gullible type with no self-awareness, but this also implies unconscious paradigms that could come up, especially on such a stressful event and a first night.

"Do you know this side of town?"

"No."

We come out of the cab as the snow stops falling. Facing us is an imposing building of several stories. Mo contemplates it with intent. I remember he studies architecture.

"You fancy the building?"

I stare at it myself with a second look; I am familiar with much of NYC and its building styles. I have favorite walks amongst salaciously constructed apartment complexes. I know some wonderful gems niched in unnamed streets between decaying buildings. Yet, before today, I didn't take in this entity as an architectural design or an object of art per se. To me, it entails much more, and so, it becomes difficult to think of it as a building or a bookstore.

"It's... It tries."

"Good enough. Follow me."

He nods and steps into the dark and narrow alley. The street lights on both sides are weak, and don't reach all the way through. We don't walk long; the secondary entrance into the bookstore is behind an unused trash bin. I open the door and carefully lead Mo through the bazaar of boxes and empty shelves. It's an improvised inventory space which hasn't been cleaned in some time. I reach out for the lamp and turn it on. Then, I take his hand and whisper:

"Are you scared?"

"N-no... Should I be?"

"Some get scared at that point. They think I want to kill them and sell their organs."

I stare at him in the dim light of the lamp with an amused expression. I see he is trying to find the humor in it, but he is nervous. Perhaps it's because of the imminence of first times, and how premeditated and slow this one is. I hope my intentionally bad jokes distract him enough that he becomes nervous about something else.

"Do you have any idea how much kidneys and a liver from someone like you would cost? And maybe not so much for their medical value, perhaps for their taste."

"I don't know..."

"I know... I know you have a delicious taste."

His face is inquisitive when I finally get to see it; in the faint lights leading to the main corridor, his bushy eyebrows, dark brown eyes, and generous mouth stand out. I don't hesitate as I firmly secure Mo and kiss him. His lack of action doesn't faze me. I take what I want, and when he finally engages, I pull back from his clumsiness.

"You taste exquisite. But you don't know how to convey it. And now, you follow me, and I will show you."

He blushes then says, in an attempt to break the tension:

"What's this place?"

What a fearful deer he makes.

"The gateway to the Love Alcove."

"What is that?"

"You'll see. Through the foreign section."

"How did you get this key?"

"By being fantastically clever and an adept sexual partner."

We reach the second floor. There is no light save for my flashlight. I know this place in and out though, and I revel in firmly holding that beautiful hand while he submits to my pace, and follows me like a lamb. It's gratifying. It's warm. It's real under my grip. If it squeezed back, it would be perfect.

"Here..."

I guide Mo beyond an aisle filled with few torn and dusty books until we reach the wall. I push the old shelf aside, and insert the key. I then hunch over to go through the small door.

"Follow me."

"Like Alice follows the rabbit?"

"Like a lamb following a shepherd."

Mo stands up as I turn on the light in the window-less and wide room; the ceiling was a vestige of some elaborate fairytale castle for children. It had been repaired without much care for the intentional shape and artistic undertones. The long curtains were improvised as a complex tent that wrapped around a sizable velvet bed. There were few trinkets from what that room used to be, but I hid most of it underneath colorful thick fabric. I always make a mental note of cleaning the place, but I never get around doing so. Throughout the day, the closed bookstore may have potential visits from prospective buyers, cleaning staff or security. I have no desire to get acquainted with new faces. Besides, the owner appreciates my discretion, just as much as I appreciate his patronage.

Mo takes a long look at the ceiling. I let him soak in the atmosphere while I turn on the lights in the room, and hastily clean up the pee bottles and the old condom wraps. The bed is neat though, and I still have some clean towels and blankets. I grab the toiletries bag I have by the bed, and head to the bathroom. It's the only place with a proper door to the hidden room, but it is assumed to be an electrical unit and is left alone. I keep it clean and use it to freshen up and be ready. I also have a bidet and a shower head there for spontaneous nights like these.

"I need to clean up. How about you?"

"I'm.... Good."

"Are you ready though? Is your hole clean?"

He is embarrassed, but I smile and gently guide him to the bathroom.

"Let me show you. There is nothing to be embarrassed about. It'll become second habit with time, like brushing your teeth."

I start taking care of myself under his hesitant stare, then he follows the motion with another bidet. I quickly shave my head and face, then freshen up. I stare at the mirror and breathe in the anticipation. When we head back, Mo is hastily checking the drawers. He speaks with a nervous tone and a more pronounced accent.

"Is there any liquor?"

"I don't like fucking pieces of meat."

I grab his hand and request his attention.

"I need you to be here and I need you to be with me when I'm with you, ok?"

Mo nods and comes closer. I bring him against me and whisper:

"There is nothing to be ready for. Get out of your own head and trust me with this dance."

He gasps for air before attempting to kiss me. I respond with more direction. When I sense his flesh getting warmer under my touch and his breathing becoming intense, I go down on him and give him a blowjob. He tries to keep quiet then let out a moan when I suck him dry. He finally let loose; kissing him indeed is provocation. Soon enough, Mo's nervousness turns into frenzy. Beyond his warmth, his energy is erratic and knows no specific routine. It would be a waste to let it expand, and a frustrating force to attempt to ride. But these are my optimal preys, and with few tweaks, they all answer to my touch. I grab the lubricant and smear my fingers. I work him up until he is relaxed. Then I take the lead.

"This will hurt, most likely. But it will get better, I promise."

He answers by seeking my lips with his, navigating my neck and bringing my face closer. I strategically engage in, controlling my desire to push. I tease him rather than penetrate him, reveling in the anticipation and my merciful control over his absolute surrender. As his body wanes on the bed, I lick the sweat out of his neck then push further.

How exquisite. I promise you pleasure and communion, Mo. Just bear it a bit more. He seems to understand and bites on my forearm, firm and harmless. I rejoice in his meaty presence and warm breath. He is all here and everything about him right now is solid coinage.

The night lasts longer than our carnal dance. By the end of my initiating performance, Mo is done groaning. He is out of breath and lying next to me. He is not a clinger. He contemplates the ceiling with wide eyes, as if it will come down on us at any time. I go to the bathroom for a quick clean up and come back to his inert figure. His body has no stamina, and his first time might have been too much despite the generous lubricant. I didn't hear a cry or a complaint through it all, but the bite marks on my arms are visible enough. I know from experience, it doesn't mean everything was smooth. But I came inside him few times, and he's had a good start for a virgin. For the next round, he is relaxed enough to be ready for another blowjob. He let me bring him to climax with my tongue and fingers.

I perform enough at this point to read and excel at understanding certain people; people in my bed, people in my audience, people staring at me, people sitting next to me. It's more of a necessity than an inherent trait of character. To survive as a sojourner with certain inclinations, within a society where threat could be disguised and present in unpredictable corners, I could only fare so long by being sharp and getting sharper. Therefore, for certain people and within certain circumstances, I'm in my territory and they give in with an inclination which follows the unspoken primitive order. They are pleased and I am satisfied. Then, by the end of the night, there will be no anticipation anymore, and certainly no attachment. With the rising sun, the burdening reality will strike the preys. Most, out of fear and uncertainty, will unequivocally remain floored. Few may give into erratic motion from the vertigo of the experience, but give it time and their infatuation will wane, and stillness will prevail.

Mo rises by my side and suddenly asks:

"You are done? Can I try?"

"I didn't know you still had something in you."

"What if I do?"

"By all means... Let me get ready then. I don't usually plan for that with a first-timer."

While I lubricate and get comfortable, Mo's stare is still hesitant. I smile at the big eyes and state, giving him a condom.

"Condom... And... Let me guide you for now... You are a rookie fairy after all, and I'd still like to enjoy myself."

Mo is smart and applied. He doesn't lose sense of himself or his control. The lack of major alcohol is to thank for that part. The awkwardness has turned into perseverance. This is serious coinage, which arouses me further. His enthusiasm doesn't match his figure and certainly not his stamina. I lock eyes with him at some point, and let him explore the sensations. Through his ecstatic eyes, I embrace my own rapture.

When he finally surrenders to his exhaustion, I keep him against me and caress his back.

"Not bad for a first time after all."

He shakes his head. Indeed.

The alarm goes off before we get any sleep. We hastily dress and I lead him to the hidden entrance.

"Go first. Only get a cab once you walked few blocks away."

"Ok, well..."

Mo is awkward and hesitant. I can't see much of him in the thin obscurity of the bookstore's first flour, and I don't need to.

"There are no pleasantries to exchange in such meetings. We're not gentlemen of the daylight, Mo. Enjoy yourself."

I hesitate to kiss him. I let him go, naturally imposing my will on my lust. He leaves and I wait sometime before I do the same.

Another Carnal Dance

Tonight, I am heading to another club to perform with the Syntho-usikeers. My bandmates are despairing of the New York scene; they were expecting to make it by now. I hide my smirk whenever they complain. I choose not to remind them, yet again, how long I have been in this game, how much I have spent of the epiphanies of my ages and the salt of my sweat performing and networking. I had knocked on every door of a progressive venue, generously introduced new wave listeners to the next best thing, and more often than not, for free. And yet, here I am, playing with a band called Syntho-usikeers while my daylight hustles pay for the tax of existence and my passion projects.

I am no better than these rats though. I have gone through that phase as well: I have believed with the same impatience, I have trodden the scenes of New York thinking of how shamefully underrated and overlooked my talent was. Unlike them however, I had calmed faster. They still entertain the raging hot blood and the vices of the rookie, and this will surely cement them in that rookie phase for the years to come. I've seen enough bands play the same single album for 20 years at the same low-level venues, and I've learnt quickly to grow, in that aspect as well, and cultivate my patience, my wits and my expertise. I got to see first-hand how intelligence was no longer the serious coinage of the poor and the meek. Perhaps, the word itself became so worn down, and full of itself that people mistake wits for whatever idiocy they nurture at this point.

From the mistakes of the fox, the wolf became clever.

Still, we have no other scene. At least I don't have to explain this simple fact to them; if we don't make it in New York, we surely won't make it anywhere else. All the stars align above the concrete version of the American dream. We head to a disco club with a stuffy atmosphere where we performed before. I don't feel the instrument tonight. It's bothersome when it happens, but I have learned to accept it. I can't control that part, so I let it go and do my best whenever I feel I have some say on the matter. It helps that I came to accept my lack of control on such circumstances, and to prepare optional material in case. On these occasions, my modified schemes and pre-recorded tracks come to the rescue, and help me deliver an earnest performance. Not that someone with a recording could swing it like I do; it takes time and the experience of having screwed it up on the scene, to develop an elegant reaction in handling the wrong turns.

Authentic music composition and music performance are rich cavalcades of the mind, filled with outlandish turns, mercurial events and unpredictable creatures. It requires cultivated vulnerability, a generosity in creation and a brave heart daring to explore ideas and face its own shortcomings. The sooner one, who calls themselves a creative, surrenders control and gets over fear, the quicker one can step into the chaos and learn to navigate it. The more one exposes themselves to a merciless audience, researches one's reactions under pressure, the better of a learning ability one develops. All that is left is to salvage insight from the embarrassment, instead of cancelling the whole experience.

To the band's annoyance, we wrap up on some requests which have nothing to do with our tracks or style. They have to accept such matters at some point, and as usual, the impatience gets the best of them. I take the opportunity to scour the audience with my enigmatic grin. A stare lingers back; I find him tacky in his USPS uniform underneath his open coat. His protruding belly and rushed beer drinking is extra points. I like that enough. Or maybe I'm in the mood of something more expeditious tonight. He doesn't waste time. He comes by while I pack my equipment.

"Hey Dorothy..."

"Not my name, but I have my fair share of handsome."

"Fancy a drink?"

"If you're buying..."

We sit down assessing each other, I more than him; the man is fairly drunk. I send a smile his way, and his naked ankles touch my leg.

"What name does this face have?"

"Josef, you?"

"Aaron. Wanna get out of here? There is this dive bar I know."

"Sounds good, but I've got a better spot. Follow me."

He scoffs at my soft order. I already know what he wants and expects. Outside, he comes close and works his hand underneath my coat. I'm not sure I like them, but the rest will do. I smile and pull away, securing his forearm with my hand and imposing the distance.

"Buddy, you will have to do better than that. But later."

"Later, huh?"

"Let's split a cab."

"I have my..."

"We're taking a cab."

"Okay lady boss, okay, okay..."

I dismiss his sloppy paradigm declaration. We'll see who will lead the carnal dance once we are at the Love Alcove. I wonder how much I could get out of a drunk fellow. His meaty build is to my delight, but he doesn't seem to be all there, which doesn't strike my fancy. Many don't like to be all there, though, and I learned to work around it. I just have to make sure he doesn't throw up or get rowdy.

"How is your testing?"

"Testing?"

"When did you get tested?"

"Psh... Who cares?"

"I do... I'm sure many don't. The night is young. You can look for them."

"I got... Tested, Josef face. Ok?"

"Where?"

"By Broadway..."

The cab stops. We both get in, though I am reticent. The idiot can't properly lie; there is no discrete testing center in Broadway. It's not so much the getting rid of the postman which bothers me, but going back to hunting grounds. I don't want to waste more money on cabs tonight.

In the taxi, he slides his hand to my thigh then my groin, while staring at me with stupid insistence. I spot the taxi driver turning his head towards the rearview mirror. This USPS idiot is the complete package. I firmly grab his wandering hand, and say through a smirk.

"You look like someone about to receive a miracle. Let me read your fortune."

"I do?"

"Let's see..."

I examine the hand, and there is not much to it. Nothing strikes me except its bad tan and fine blond hair. There is the obvious white circle around his ring finger, but it's common.

"I see... Push your head so I can see. I see a scorned wife who cheats on her partner, some children who are more like dolls than children. I see plenty of money from an injury that won't be so serious. Hm money from there on... Lucky you, Aaron. You will remember your poor friends when you become rich, right?"

"Yeah, yeah... But what's that about my wife cheating on me?"

What an idiot. From there until we get to destination, I ask him about his children. Then, I talk about my own, the fictional ones I have woven along the encounters, and who came to have a life of their own, so that talking about them is effortless, lively and a decent means of contraception with the likes of Aaron.

When we come out of the taxi, the postman is pretty awkward from the conversation. But his drunken ass takes one look at my secure figure, and stands tall and proud.

"I guess we should call it a night, Aaron. Go to your children and I'll go to mine."

"What? I'm here already! And you are here... And you look like you really need something inside you. I promise I'm..."

"There is no testing center in Broadway, not for you or for me. I liked you enough, but that's where I draw the line. Go home to your wife and kids."

The postman doesn't care much for the public place, and immediately shoves me against the streetlight. I was expecting the reaction and have put my instrument next to me. I let him get the upper hand. He buries his head in my neck, and tries to undo his pants. What a dynamite idiot, and under the streetlight of all the places. He whispers in frenzy.

"Listen pretty mouth, I'm sure you want this just as much as I do. It'll be quick, we will wrap it..."

"And I said no monkey business..."

He finally disengages while I press the razor against his neck. I am no longer the polite and soft-spoken witty man from the techno bar with the European crowd. I am no longer the suave player who is indulging some aggressive foreplay. Now, it's the Josef who learned how to handle a knife, to play with a razor just as good as he plays his synthesizer. To make it in the concrete jungle implies a compulsory drive to survive with the top of the food chain. It implies being smart about the use of deviance and vice. No one is making it in the Wicked City without a fair share of intelligent deviance, and a synergy with one's demons.

"Get lost now, before I cut you deep enough... That'll keep you from working and fucking."

He tries to fight, but I mercilessly push him away. He falls on the floor, and has a debilitated look on his face as he stares at me. He is too drunk to process everything, but knows enough not to attempt something with someone who reads violence.

"Now, you fuck off..."

"You fucking fag..."

I menacingly reach for something in my pocket, and he sets off in a clumsy pace. I grab my instrument and head towards the hidden door, turning my back to the postman, but keeping my ears on the job. I trust them better than my eyes, and there is no use showing weakness or a sign of fear at this point. The moment I turn around into the dark alley, I hear a gasp and I instantly get my razor out and on the neck of the dark silhouette.

"Sorry... Sorry! It's me, it's me..."

I have trouble recognizing the full figure.

"It's Mo! I'm sorry! I didn't mean to scare you..."

The adrenaline is in my system. As a consequence, I ask without thinking:

"What the fuck are you doing here?"

I look at the street, make sure Aaron is no longer in sight. I look at Mo again, now ready for some warped excuse. Why was he there indeed? I had made it clear enough he was the affair of one night.

"I didn't know how to get in touch with you, aside from here."

His accent is back. I disengage. I inhale for some time with a disapproving stare, letting him stew in his nervousness. He shouldn't get any ideas.

"The bartender of The Welle said you guys performed often but he didn't have your contact, and didn't know when the Syntho ... When your band would be back... That's your band, right?"

"..."

"So, I thought, just... Give it a try... Wait here, maybe?"

"What are you doing here, Mo?"

I didn't like being outside in the open next to one of my hookup locations. This is the sort of events triggering the curiosity of people who have no headaches to keep them away from others' affairs. This old industrial quarter didn't have many of those. But New York's gentrification is rapid enough that I wouldn't be surprised folks with more money and time than the usual residents would be around.

I drag Mo to the darkness by the side entrance. He jumps on my neck after a moment of hesitation, and I push him against the wall. I appreciate the gesture, but not like this, and not under messy circumstances. The puppy is learning though, and it pleases me enough to cast aside my irritation.

"No... You don't get to do anything. Answer me first... What are you doing here?"

I'm guessing he didn't fend well for himself after our night together. Perhaps he is getting attached; highly uncommon but I could understand. Still, I thought I was being clear.

"You don't strike me as the package of the absolute herb. You didn't think this would go anywhere now, did you?

Mo shakes his head and says after a moment of hesitation:

"No, no... But I... I want my fill."

"What?"

"You got yours, didn't you? I want my satisfaction..."

I scoff, almost relieved yet amazed at the foreign confidence of the non New Yorker. The entitlement is almost realistic and well rooted, in the spirit of the American confidence. I don't usually get that from my prey.

"You have complaints?"

"No, just that it wasn't enough. And I think from a transactional point of view, you got what you wanted, but I didn't. And I think we both want the same thing, and I think you are alone tonight, and I think we could both make use of the night and the company."

I nod with a smirk. The attitude delights me. I step away and look around, listening with intent to potential company. There is no one else. The postman is long gone. Mo was confident while giving his little speech, but now he is staring at me with his puppy eyes, his hands dangling like sticks by his side.

"Fair enough. As long as everything is crystal clear. I don't want a puppy."

"That would be an insult to me."

"The way you were waiting here makes me think otherwise."

"I had no other choice."

"What? No luck with other strangers?"

He shrugs and waits for me to make a move. I unlock the door and motion with my head. Why the hell not? There is nobody else tonight. Besides, the altercation with Aaron left my blood bumping. The adrenaline had to go. What better way to spend it than with someone who openly admits to wanting his fill? I never get complaints, but I seldom meet the same person more times, let alone to the extent where they are comfortable enough about giving me feedback. There are few movements in this concert. If each does his part correctly, both of us are satisfied, and each goes on their merry way. And I happen to think I fuck well and fair on a normal day. Additionally, if I get something to work with or I'm in the zone, I am a demented sexual wonder.

Once we get into the Love Alcove, Mo wastes no time; he aggressively kisses me and I follow along, amused by his ferocity. I'm fairly confident he won't be able to sustain the tension. His hands run too fast on my body that I don't get to commit his touch to flesh or memory.

The turbulence provokes my mind, and incites me to take over. Mo is relentless and eventually exhausted. I grant him a breather while I clean myself and shave my head. I'm back and we proceed again, this time with me leading the carnal dance, reteaching him all that I guided him through before. There is much to register and enjoy in our physical partnership, except for when I lose focus at times. This is some serious coinage. What a beautiful bastard.

When the alarm goes off, Mo is reluctant to move. I don't spare him.

"We need to leave. Now."

"I know."

I quickly improvise a wash and put on my clothes. He follows with a slower pace. Before we leave the room, however, he holds me back and says:

"Can I get a number?"

"Of what?"

"Some address? How to get in touch with you?"

I don't give into such requests. The only people who can afford reliable sex should have their own keys to provide, and should be beyond the scope of worry. None of which applies to this rookie fairy so far. Besides, I want no one to know I don't have a landline, that I live in Harlem, or that I have four roommates. I scoff and say:

"Why? Waiting by the empty bookstore isn't cutting it for you?"

"It'll make it easier..."

"Then, look for someone who will make it easier. Just make sure to use a condom."

I hesitate for half a second, not wanting to bring up the topic yet feeling the need to clarify to the foreigner. I then state:

"AIDS is everywhere. If you're not careful, you will direly regret your humping session."

"I heard... But, when do we meet here then?"

I smile while answering:

"That's a great question."

Mo smiles back. I don't know if he is at ease or he just likes my smile. I don't want to know, though. I don't care.

"Let's put it this way. If by any chance, some day, I come around the same night hour and I find you, we can go inside to fuck."

He doesn't understand or doesn't want to. I motion for him to follow and we head to the exit.

"So which day?"

"Any... Don't try to force the door, though, or bring someone here, or any monkey business that is... You really don't want to have any monkey business with me. You got that?"

"Yes."

"You come whenever you want and I come whenever I want. If both of us happen to be here and to be alone, why not? Bear in mind I might not be alone. In such case, I'm not sure whether the other guy would like you to join. Would it be something you are interested in?"

He is stunned by my statement. I give him some time to process, then wait on an answer.

"I'm not sure."

"Well... Think about it for next time, and we'll see if the other player would join in."

Mo nods in some sort of unsettled agreement. Before I let him leave, I grab him and kiss him properly; deep enough to bring back the memories of the night, light enough to let the causality of the daylight settle as well.

Mo is confused and flushed. But then, he reaches out to my groin without hesitation. I let him follow his whim before we hastily take care of each other in the moldy inventory space.

"Hope you had your fill now."

"Not really."

"You've come to the right place then."

I let Mo leave and think of the night: I sense a certain kinship with the guy, at least in our approach to lust and to quenching the human instinct. In him, I can sense a potential to be a generous and applied sexual partner. I'm a great teacher after all and a great sex practitioner myself. Is this what it feels like to be in a clear agreement with a fellow hunter? I stop following this line of thought. I'm getting ahead of myself. Who knows whether Mo will turn up next time, or will engage in the carnal dance with the same intentions?

Maybe he will get discouraged. Maybe the daylight will hit him hard this morning, and he would actually crawl back to the comforting shame, and the boxed reality he is doomed to have. Multiple reasons could align, and finally make him see beyond the fleeting pleasures of the night. Multiple reasons could form brick walls, and he would most likely not deconstruct.

Deconstruction is a tough job. It comes out of necessity and being pushed into it. The few who willingly engage with it are rare and invisible. I'm not expecting this one Middle Eastern man to be the exception to the rule. As long as everything is clear, and I get to enjoy his body and he gets to have his fill, there is nothing more to it. There should be no plan, in no way, shape or form, associated with carnal dances of our kind.

Ménage à Trois

For two weeks, I dismiss the Love Alcove. I meet an old partner at his city threeplex, and we have other brands of sex. After a private get-together held at Mama's townhouse, I accompany the drunk manager to his hotel room, and meet a fine receptionist who spends his break with me. I am my usual assured self: Whether it works out or not, I am confident I have someone else or will find the next one. I rejoice in the fulfilled rapture as much as in the butchered flirt sessions. Both heighten my instinct and mind in different ways. Both are healthy components of a realistic diet. Besides, I don't like to commit my flesh to something that has no serious coinage. It's years now since I had an issue rejecting some pretenders, stopping amidst the heat of the foreplay, or pulling away. I provide more and request no less, and I learned how to beg while in control. If I am begging, it's because I'm already getting it. The question is just the execution, and how coordinated and artistic I want it at that moment.

Despite the cold winter and the wind, my mother doesn't skip our monthly walks in Central Park. They grow shorter with the sun motion. She still manages to complain about my absence during Christmas, my weight, and my sparse phone calls. She asks about work and girlfriends, and I ask about neighbors, radio stations and current reading material. It is a short and nice afternoon mother-son date, but it brightens my mood and brings some emotional stability to a physically spent creature. Sunset is upon us. She wants us to push further, but I refuse that she walks around Central and New York in darkness. I call her a cab despite her protests. I don't want my mother's presence to be part of my nightlife.

Past 11 p.m., after some drinks with good folks and friends, I go back to the bookstore building. I see no one, but I hear a car unlock. I head to the dark alley, and scrutinize its exits. Surely enough, it was Mo. There is a possibility he was the one coming out of the car. He is next to me but keeps his distance. He learns and, needless to say, it delights me and makes me yearn for his hands. But I don't let lust mess with my focus. There is no room for idiotic gestures in this relationship, or any of my relationships for that matter.

I open the door and he steps inside. Soon enough, Mo is ready and openly offers himself. Ah, the acceptance in surrender, the honest vulnerability. All such solid coinage. It pushes all the right buttons in me, swallows me in a state of feverish anticipation. I am allowed full range without precautions, anxiety and nervousness management. The gratification is beyond the act itself. It is, once more, worth the patience invested in these early embraces.

Much like building a melody, I am acquainted with the basics. I know the technicalities, and I elegantly bring them into place where needed. But it's the inspiration that guides me through the main process, the focal loadings, the points of tension, the harmonic movement and the locking on the zone where every touch is felt throughout the whole body. I want Mo begging for relief, and I want my body to fill on his presence and internalize it.

When his turn comes, he is dismantled and clumsy. I admire the effort, and still guide him through another route, other ways to have sex, to enjoy ourselves and to de-escalate the tension without burning too fast. In the end, he is slightly shivering.

"I ... I ... I still feel you deep. You didn't leave."

"I tend to do that..."

"This was beyond anything I ever..."

"Don't get too hung up on it. You just got to know what good sex is. That's all."

He shakes his head, as if in disbelief.

"Somebody ever... Fucked you this way?"

I don't like the question.

"Get some rest. Otherwise, if you have a mouth to talk, you have a mouth to use."

He stares at the ceiling with his wide eyes, while I grab his hand and stare at it in a rising rapture; I don't know what I want exactly to do with it. At this point, Mo would let me do anything, absolutely anything with his hands. Yet I don't know what to do with them, or what I want from them. I never truly grasped this fascination I have with hands. I don't know whether it's something from my youth, or some unfathomable kink an absurd reality had bestowed upon me. Come to think of it, one of the main reasons I became an artist was my fascination with dexterous hands and their capacity at creating something glorious out of thin air.

I need to get it together. We should sleep at this point. Mo still stares at the ceiling, and doesn't mind my fingers interlaced with his. I state, clearly to break some bizarre momentum threatening to build up:

"Next time, I'm most likely bringing someone."

"Ok."

"If you're not fine with it, better don't show up for some days."

"What about him? Will he be fine with it?"

"Beats me."

He stares at me, and says in surprise:

"You don't know him?"

I scoff:

"Of course not. It depends on who the night brings along."

"What if he doesn't want to..."

"Then he's free to walk away..."

We are quiet for some time. I'm feeling sleepy.

"How do you do that?"

"What?"

"I mean... If I were to be on the verge of getting some-one, I wouldn't want to upset them with anything. I'd really like to fuck them. I would do or say anything, until I get at least a good fucking out of them. I don't think I could ever do the opposite once I'm set on someone. You know: 'I want to fuck you, but hold on! Let me tell you something that might come in the way'... That, Josef, I don't think I could ever do that."

His honesty is always interesting to witness. It's so foreign that I get lost staring at him while processing the words he admits to with ease.

"Maybe you should start doing that. It will make your life surprisingly easier. That, I vouch for."

"I don't know... I'm too scared of going back home alone. If I get rejected multiple times, I am afraid I will believe it will always be the case, even though it's not the reality, but..."

"Is that why you came back? You can't put yourself out there?"

"... Maybe..."

"You're young. You have your whole life and this whole city. Once you get over your fear, you will see for yourself... Getting screwed isn't the issue in New York, it's the opposite."

"Are you sure?"

"I don't need to be sure."

I don't like the conversational tone and the direction of the discussion. I turn my back to him, and close my eyes.

Mo is silent for a moment. He then says.

"Are you done already?"

"You're the one out of it."

"I'm back in."

He wants to give, and I let him do so without reticence. If anything, I'm pleasantly surprised by his commitment to fairness, and his eagerness to give back. That is if Mo thinks he can achieve it.

Why not? I am patient, and my carnal nights are just for that. Whether the time is all spent in impeccable fucking, half-decent rounds, miserable taps or clumsy attempts, I'm game. I learned to appreciate the nights for what they bring, and the occasional great fuck here and there. This one is here for now, trying and improving. Few things he has no control over, but the will is there. And if he sticks around, soon enough, he will champion few tricks, and it will be priceless coinage. These thoughts keep me going with equal levels of presence and dedication.

I yet have to come by the abandoned bookstore and not find Mo. He is getting better at the carnal dance. It seem to be his main motivation. I happen to enjoy the mentoring, and also the harvest in the following nights. He is a promising sex pietist. Should he control his inclination to talk, and be better at coordinating his movements, I would find our seances optimal. But our breaks from the physical embrace make Mo talkative.

Perhaps it's a good thing to have after all. It's a great reminder of the mental distance required, and the delicate balance which could easily be lost. Let it be lost, just not so recklessly. I wouldn't mind the bottle of Soviet champagne pouring on the floor. But I would certainly not kick it to the ground either. Let it stand on its own inertia. Let Mo move to the whims of his desire. Much of it brings me delight and gratification, and the rest is the optimal contraception to keep the individual into the box of sexual partnership.

Tonight is the night then. I bring another one to the dance. While I almost drag the fearful deer inside, Mo joins us from behind, startling the newcomer. I reassure him as he hesitantly looks behind, and can't discern the face of Mo.

"You were joking right there, sir? Right?"

"Yes, Saeed... And if you relax, you'll enjoy my humor better."

We get to the room. Mo is by Saeed's side, who is shorter and muscular. His beard is well groomed. His eyelashes are thick and long. He is a fine specimen. I know from Mo's stares he is comparing himself to Saeed. I contemplate letting them stew together for some time while I take care of myself. It will be interesting to figure out this ménage, and how to guide it.

The experiment is intriguing enough. The outcome would be something fresh to figure out. Increasing the complexity and figuring out the optimal paradigms don't often happen under one's consent. This is a luxurious opportunity.

As they stay together in the room, I carefully shave my head and listen. What could two birds of similar feathers who actively avoid their own kind duet about? My smirk turns into a scoff. I stare at myself in the mirror. I am satisfied and head back to the room.

"Gentlemen of the night, shall we do this?"

Saeed frenetically nods, while Mo assesses the situation with a cool attitude.

"Mo, if you are not comfortable with the arrangement, feel free to leave. Saeed is in. Right?"

I ask as I make my way to the middle of the bed and relax, waiting for the rest to unfold. Mo finally says:

"I'm okay with it. I just don't know..."

"You're in luck. That's one of the good things about me."

Saeed asks, more to be part of the conversation and shed his nervousness than to know.

"One of the good things?"

"One of many, sir. Come here."

"Do you have any drink?"

"I don't fuck bland meat. I like my human awake and present... See Saeed, I'm here to fuck 'you', not the rest. I'm here to fuck you, for as long as convenient, for as much as we like. So, no drinking on the hedonistic duty. Only before. Perhaps after too, if it was that bad. I promise you, though, it won't be. Not with me."

I open my arms, and motion for him to come. Saeed is the first to obey. I take care of his clothes and flip him on his stomach. It seems I don't need to tell Mo anything; he's behind me already. This will prove to be a delightful evening. I follow with Mo while robbing Saeed of his breath, his nervousness and his strength. He is a moaner. I have to silence him at times. It quickly becomes a feverish affair that I guide in the tempestuous amalgam of bodies with the intoxication of a lustful sea captain.

Ahab didn't want to kill God. He wanted to fuck it. Right now, we all want to fuck God, oh so badly. Unlike these two, I don't want to do so in one setting, 'get it out of my system', 'make room in life for something else'. I make it last, I am patient, I let it linger. I promise you God, it will be slow and painful, and I will drag it for as long as I fancy. There is nothing more absurd than this life, and I am not about to 'move on', and make sense of it, find meaning. I create it at every turn I decide. I dismiss it altogether when I fancy.

Mo's presence is strong. His musk pervades, and intensifies my pleasure. He's come some way at this point. He switches with Saeed, and Saeed doesn't know any better. He will certainly not be able to take me, and he has no strength either. Whatever he has been building up in his torso is nonexistent in his hips and legs. He is by our side heavily breathing as I give Mo what he demands. I push him beyond the limits we've explored, then some more for decorum. Saeed clings to us. I bring him underneath and pleasure them both. He is clumsy with Mo, and Mo responds prismatically to the fluid and sloppy motion. I understand he is trying to impose some structure, and I can't help but smile: It takes more than knowing how to fuck to have such refined movement, my sex pietist. It takes attitude well outside the bed and the intercourse. And I'm suspecting Mo is figuring it out just now.

In the middle of the bed, Saeed snores. Mo comes back from the bathroom with an odd glare. I was hoping I could sleep, but I remember that if I stay quiet, he might start talking again. He comes back to bed. I whisper to him, the stranger between us.

"Are you not satisfied?"

"No."

"Care to join me in the bathroom then?"

"I'd like here and now."

I get up and come by his side of the bed. Through Mo's indecisive glance, I discern his turbulent thoughts; he doesn't know whether he likes it, whether he would be up for a ménage à trois next time. Under such circumstances, it's wise to bring back stability, first and foremost. It could come in the shape of reassurance, and it is reassuring to grant some power, or at least the illusion of it. I stare around me, and ask in a whisper:

"Do you want me on the bed?"

I slide to the floor, improvising an odalisque pose, and I lift my head to stare at him.

"Or here on the floor?"

He is quizzical for a moment, then tries to hide his surprise. I crawl to come near his face.

"Maybe you want me here, Mo?"

I extend my legs and level my head by his thighs.

"Or here?"

At his indecision, I pass a hand on my short and ask:

"Perhaps this is all you want me to do? Right here?"

He shakes his head, and crosses his hands. I look away, refusing to be distracted.

"What will it be then, Mo? What would it take for you to get your fill? We have the rest of the night, but nothing more."

He finally admits.

"I don't know."

That's all I need to hear. I grab his hands, kiss them profusely and state:

"Good thing that I do."

"You do what?"

"That I know."

"You do know, Josef.... You really do."

I kiss his torso as he seems to internalize the notion that I, indeed, do know. I take him in methodically. This time, I let in voracious appetites. They take over me. I become unbothered by rough play at this point. Mo seems to like it, wants me to push further with vengeance. That self-destructive instinct is ugly and sickening, but I'm neither a doctor nor a messiah. I'm not about to change anybody's life. Most harbor the sickness, let it fester within, become uglier from it and treat it as a new normal. Few catalyze the sickness, and a handful acknowledge its roots and try to treat it. I know what such mental state in a sexual partner could grant me, but I'm no pig either. I will take few fine cuts, then leave him to his devices. There is no saving that brand of people from such behavior. Mo is not just surrendering, he begs for utter destruction. His attitude and resistance are gone. I promise you, Mo. You won't come out of this the same sort of dead. And perhaps, you will wish to be dead again.

By dawn, we are leaving. Mo describes the road to Saeed towards the closest bus station. Once the guy disappears, he turns to me and asks.

"What was that supposed to mean?"

I sense the constipated anger. There are several matters he could take issue with at this point. I decide to cut it short. On one hand, I'm not up for an emotional outburst or a tantrum. On the other hand, I'd like to single out the reason as soon as possible. Getting into layered conversations requires a brand of intelligence that I'm not sure Mo has.

"Nothing... As usual. It was getting down between adults."

"No, not that part."

"You'll have to help me out here. Which part should have meant something in the first place then?"

"Why him? Why Saeed? Why bring Saeed?"

"I told you: I never know the stranger I'm about to meet."

"Yet, you manage to bring someone like Saeed."

"Someone who happened to venture, out of pure curiosity of course, on the right side of Chelsea. Someone who heard of some underground clubs that are 'safe', and where there are no 'rats, only Dorothies'? Someone decided to check it out? Someone no one wanted to take home because the magic klink klink of money doesn't go with his brown skin and Arabian looks? Someone awkward enough to be on his own and nurse one drink after the other while he reads virgin and lonely closeted bastard to every gay and desperate New Yorker who would ironically go to such places to check the scene? Someone like that? Yes! Saeed has a tiny edge though: He happened to like my music."

He tries to find something to say back, but he is at loss of words, or perhaps too angry to articulate his thought.

"Are you angry?"

"A little. There is something really messed up about bringing that man."

"I warned you."

"I don't like it, Josef."

"Then next time, you know what to do."

He scowls at me and I maintain my composed and regal attitude.

"Where is he from anyway?"

"Saudi Arabia... I think it's close to that 'here and there' place."

He is about to leave, but I retain him, forcefully.

"Hey. We may be nothing but fuck buddies, but I was joking to lighten your mood. I tell you, there is no meaning to anything. Don't read too much into it. It'll be nothing but a growing pit of disappointment."

I loosen my grip. He is not so willing to leave anymore, but he still has a dark stare. It's lovely to see a new shade of emotions on such pronounced dark features.

"Or maybe you could read too much into it, and choose not to turn up here anymore, which is something I would understand and respect. But at least, you've got a potential new companion."

"Is that the point?"

"What did I tell you? There is no meaning. There is no point. But since you insist on finding something, there it goes... After all, even though we are messed up circus freaks in many aspects according to this world, we do

look out for each other in strange and convoluted ways...
What say you?"

"I don't know what made you like this, Josef. I'm not sure whether you are an incredibly clever or an incredibly sad man."

"Or maybe both..."

"Or maybe both. But I didn't... I assumed everything is clear between us and there would be no need for such 'games'..."

"You've made your voice heard. No more group sex for you."

"It's not about that... Josef, I want the same thing than you. I want to be free, and get my fill, and then move on with my life. Don't you want the same?"

I smile and nod. There is no reason to nurture an existential dialogue.

"Then why do you keep being so aloof once the deed is done? And then bring someone like Saeed into the mix?"

"Who I am and what I am shouldn't be a concern or a point of discussion in the first place."

"But it's..."

"And if who I am as a human is bringing you any offense, then please, feel free to leave and never look back. This has always been about the sexual experience for me, nothing more."

"I'm... You're... Josef, I'm not coming for you... Either... I'm just saying that you don't need to be like that with me. I already know what I'm getting, and what I want. I talk to you for instance and you..."

"And I don't listen. I don't care. I don't want to know."

I stop to recollect. I rely on my deep breaths to regulate my mood. It's the morning after an intense night. Situations easily escalate on empty stomachs, weary bodies and heavy minds. I resume, intending to end this exchange.

"If your idea of self-preservation involves being talkative and open, the least you could do is acknowledge it's not the same for the rest of us."

"I know, I know..."

"You're in New York City. We're both partaking in something exclusively carnal. Whatever you internalized or picked up from here and there will neither apply to this place nor to me."

Mo listens and understands. He inhales deeply and exhales for long. I'd like to reward him with a kiss, but it's tricky right now. I throw him a bone:

"I like fucking you. I assume you like fucking me too. But if it stops being an enjoyable experience, we stop it. If you are not comfortable with threesomes, you say so. There is nothing worth fighting for, nothing worth overlooking. Think about it and make your own decision."

Mo is hesitant as he nods. He then leaves. I need to take my mind off this altercation now. I look forward to the demanding daylight commitments. I even shuffle few things to pour my attention into something and somebody else for now. I don't think about delicate and tricky matters right after they happen. I need them to settle first. I need to be sharp and ready for when they are stable enough in my mind.

Sweet Rapture of Lust and Music

I wrap up a performance at an underground club while discreetly scouring the dance floor. There has been no one new and delightful enough to make the cut and be my guest so far. I haven't gone to the Love Alcove in some time. I briefly toyed again with the notion of expanding my hunting ground despite the lack of benefits to such an action: Beyond the multiple and stupid risks of such venture, the fact remains that going beyond Chelsea and the underground gay scene means an absence of awareness over testing, no standard protection use as well as an increased and desolate level of junkies and mentally ill individuals barely able to function. It becomes much more challenging to find people equally minded over simple basics. You will have more luck getting your dick sucked and your fucking going though. The catch is that it will be a junkie, and I have never been into fucking the mentally disabled and hollow shells of flesh. I leave that to the insecure and the desperate. I like my preys optimal, with backbone and fangs to them.

I am aware of that. It doesn't mean I don't slip at times, especially when velveteen trash slips into a retro scene made blinding by neon lights. Aggressive encounters can start at the dance floor. An initial contact, a flirtatious look and a fight erupts. Scratches, cuts or bruises happen. Last one for instance was a miscalculation from my end. I failed to recognize the addict behind the hyperactivity on the dancefloor, and got out of it after few fists. One landed on my temple, and bruised the corner of my eye. This is not a great look for the daylight's commitments, but I manage with some makeup and with less professional and friendly visits.

The guitarist is moving away and leaving the band. I take over the instrument while we find someone to replace him. My synthesizer tracks are ready anyway, and I don't mind them doing the work for few gigs. While we are playing, I see Mo getting to the closest table and sitting down with a drink. He listens with intent. I can't help but smile; I wonder whether this is a move. What does it matter? I don't care.

We wrap up the show, give way to the next band. I entrust the guitar to the guys, then head to the bar and grab a beer. Mo is still by his table, most likely scribbling in his notebook. Will he join me? Or take it as a power play and expect me to join him? Both prospects amuse me. What if I walk away and let him enjoy another underground experience from the next retro wave band? I chuckle while drinking and staring at his head.

I join Mo and state with a smile:

"Of all the nights to listen to us play, you come at the worst possible one."

He smiles back and says:

"Perhaps this is why I liked it better this time?"

"Perhaps... It's certainly not some sort of jazz, though."

"Ah! I should have requested jazz."

"Anything but jazz."

He leans over and whispers:

"I'd love to hear you play some jazz."

I lean closer and answer with a smile:

"I guarantee you it's the one thing you will never hear me play."

Mo shakes his head, and mutters something foreign.

"Did you sigh in another language?"

"More or less..."

"Inconsiderate..."

I catch the contours of a building on a notebook by his side. He hastily puts it away then gives me the eye. He wants us to leave.

"You mean you didn't come for the show?"

"I'd rather do something else."

"Tsk... You have no idea what you are missing. This is the sound of the future, and we are pioneering it from the boroughs of the Dirty Apple. You will look back at this time when your grandchildren will listen to nothing else but synthetic waves, and you will tell them: 'Back in my days, music made us question what we feel, it wasn't the means to create a feeling. You live even less than I did and I wasn't even living'..."

Mo scoffs.

"That's harsh."

"Be grateful. You will be having grandkids in this future."

"And you won't?"

It's time to leave. I smile and stand.

"Shall we head outside?"

The night is rich with throes of passion. The touch is gentle, the appetite voracious. I think Mo is coming into his own sensuality. I could feel him more present against me. Did he put on weight or was he inhabiting his body better? The clumsiness is replaced with a personal coordination of his own. He knows how to breathe, and when to rest. He brings his own tempo and a painfully sweet rapture to the sexual carnage. I'm extremely gratified. He doesn't talk. I understand it's a conscious choice and I let him be. We wrap up early, both spent and relaxed. I think this is the first night we've had a deep sleep.

In the morning, Mo asks me before leaving:

"Hey, don't read too much into it. But would you like to have breakfast together?"

"Depends on where..."

"There is a diner few blocks away."

"That would be a greasy spoon, not a diner."

"Does it matter?"

"Depends who is paying too."

"I am... ?"

"What's the occasion?"

"Nothing really. I'm done with few projects. It's the semester break. I have time. I can afford to grab a real breakfast. You either want to join or not."

I assess his offer and nod. There is no harm indeed. We sit down and he orders a hearty breakfast. I order a coffee and soft scrambled eggs. I am in the mood for more, but I'm not about to eat something messy or be at ease in here. The waitress is overworked and absent-minded enough, but I don't like the stares of the cook and I hope the coffee is at least prepared outside of the kitchen. I examine the man at the payment counter and zero in on the place's culture; I think we are fine, but better be careful. Mo smiles at me for no reason, and I maintain a stoic face. When we get our orders, I discreetly examine my eggs and sip the coffee.

Mo doesn't talk, contrary to the usual. The waitress had practically thrown the plates in front of him, and he gave her a warm smile in response. He then started gobbling down his pancakes. I, on the other hand, stare at his hand, nonchalant and lying next to his cup of coffee. I think of my mother and I am disturbed. Maybe it's time to pay her a visit in Downtown Village after all. Am I getting too soft, or is there a dead cat on the line? I don't understand what's about Mo's hands that remind me of her.

The sun is slowly coming up, illuminating the greasy spoon. At times, Mo glances at me and I let him be at ease while worrying about our surroundings. The establishment is old and moldy. I doubt there would be much business for it on that desolate side of the district. Whoever can afford to eat outside will probably not come here. The walls' paint is peeling off. Some tiles of the floor are broken, and the cleaning is more than questionable. I'm not sure whether it's just a safety issue at this point, or a hygiene one as well. Mo doesn't seem to mind at all. I don't expect him to care. He doesn't understand these streets yet. I hear his voice softly say, his head pointing outside of the windows:

"I came to New York to be free. I underestimated how oppressive the streets would be, how tacky the concrete will feel. It's the craziest thing! The environment became a burden I didn't expect, the most oppressive part."

"Or maybe you are over it all..."

"Over what?"

"You're through the honeymoon period with the illusion... You are through with the idea of American Freedom and not quite ready to face the reality. So, you're channeling the mourning through your personal outlets."

"Personal outlets?"

"Architecture... Buildings. Urban development. Whatever it is you do for studies."

"You remembered."

"Of course."

"I thought you didn't listen."

"Just when you babble your way onto the next round. I find it a turnoff."

Mo scoffs and looks at me, then my intertwined fingers.

"Maybe it's the light, but you look softer in the morning."

"..."

"I always wondered what you looked like in the morning... What you would feel like if I met you on the streets in the afternoon... What sort of person you are when you work, or fill up paperwork, or engage in conversations without any walls."

"You've got time on your hand."

"Not really, but it keeps me engaged."

"As long as it's in your head, enjoy it for both of us. That was some crappy coffee and pathetic eggs. Let me never catch you eating at this place again."

He asks, pointing to my temple:

"Was that always there?"

"It's nothing. It will fade away with time."

I put my hand against my face, and give him a smile of reassurance. He shakes his head while stating:

"It's crazy to me that I can't even tell whether it's a cut or a birthmark, if it was there before or came to be now... I thought I saw it yesterday, but I didn't want to embarrass myself or you, in case you always had it or something."

"It's fine. Nothing crazy about it. We are strangers to each other after all."

I know it's not necessary to remind him. But at such times, I think it's important; it asserts the boundaries of our ménage, and centers back the conversation to less intimate spaces. Mo sighs. I initiate a move to take my leave.

"How did it happen... If you don't mind me asking?"

"Some are up for something at times. And I don't de-escalate the situation as efficiently."

"But this could be dangerous."

"That's part of it."

"That doesn't sound right to me. What part in seeking pleasure or hooking up with people should come with danger?"

I scoff at the gullible man facing me. Despite his thick beard and brows, his deer eyes and mouth translate more inexperience than maturity. I am a tutor and a mentor, by practice and through skills. I could use my patience and wits to walk him through it, or I could just let him do some critical thinking on his own.

"I sound like a herb to you, don't I?"

"Indeed. Dealing with the Other inherently comes with a risk. Is that something you don't already have in your toolset of common sense?"

He shrugs and remains quiet. I add:

"And dealing with the Other in the context of intimacy, pleasure, taboo and unarticulated expectations and thoughts adds dense complicated layers to it. Dealing with the Other is more often than not a gamble. Americans have been trying to make the process easier, whether by molding some ground rules, breaking and crafting interactions down through some pseudo-science, or molding the Other into specific blocks, each coming with a manual. And whoever doesn't fit the description will not come with a manual, and is to be disregarded altogether. The essential idea through it all is to make interacting with the Other an asepticized, mapped and boxed experience. But it will always be a gamble, especially with outliers of society like us. Whether the Other ceases to become a stranger on some level doesn't declaw them altogether."

His stare has become sharp, as if he is narrowing on the meaning behind what I just said. I'm unfazed and push the coffee cup away. He suddenly asks:

"How do you do it?"

"Do what?"

"Know how to deal with the Other..."

"Practice and intelligence. I interact with people, actively... Proactively... I don't cease interacting with strangers, sensing the pulse of places, observing the audience, assessing the comings and goings."

"It sounds effortless coming from you..."

"It's practice... Mandatory practice."

I weigh my words, then add:

"Skipping such practice is luxury. Solitude and isolation are the stuff of money. So is keeping up to the properly labelled Others who answer to specific expectations, adhere to particular guidelines. If you're poor and didn't learn early on the basics of dealing with different people, you will end up in a sorrowful state, or on the streets blaming your unbelievable misfortune."

I smile and take my leave as soon as the golden rays permeate the streets and give New York an elegant hue it has no business wearing. I like that smooth start of the day. This morning though, I wonder whether there is more to it than the intimate satisfaction within the moment; something trying to extend its wings to other parts of my life. I leave it all at the greasy spoon, dismiss it altogether as the motions of daylight living take over.

I head to Greenwich Village after a tutoring session to generate elements for my tracks. I had managed to save enough for a five-hour rental of the studio. Mama doesn't meet me this time, which is not uncommon. Her assistant, Miss Otish, welcomes me. She handles the fees and guides me to the studio while making small talk. She is not as much of a recluse as Lady Mama, but her friendly and unauthentic manners speak of the little time she has for interactions. She is a fantastic assistant, and had been by the side of Mama for more than seven years.

"I will leave you to it. Mama may come by later. As usual, don't mind her. She'll just want to attend the process in silence."

"The usual."

In trying to get in touch with a well-renowned avant-garde label manager, I was referred to, then introduced to Mama, whom I didn't know at first from her persona, but rather through her early works. She had come in the early 50s to the U.S. from an obscure corner of Europe, and created a radical movement in synthetic pop under a dead name. I was already at silent awe at her body of work and artistic prowess. But I didn't realize how privileged I was to be on a first-name basis, until I stepped into her confined property, and got to speak to her outside of private parties and money talks. Mama is an ethereal creature who has the consistency of air at this point. She is over people in general, and cares solely about her poodles and her absent creativity.

I suspect underneath the thin skin and frail bones, there is a feverish artist waiting for a decade now to share something with the world. Presently though, she could only share her personalized Moog and hardware setup with a select few. Her whole studio is a wonder of technology she designed, engineered and improved upon all by herself, while waiting for her artistic block to be lifted. I'm allowed to make use of the facilities at times, provided I'm not unnerved by her peculiar energy and vague stare whenever she wants to be present. It doesn't faze me, not because I know what is behind Mama's eyes, but because she is Mama: We'd trust her if she grew razor teeth and asked us to walk inside her gaping mouth.

In the evening, I acknowledge the weariness of my body and my soul. I know better than to pair up music composition at the studio, and music performance at the tacky lobby hotel. The combo of what I am consumed doing versus what I prostitute for the sake of those few hours in Greenwich Village plays a number on my mind. It swarms it with noise and confusing thoughts. Yet, when it's past seven in the evening, I head to the hotel. I put on a smile, gather some energy within to spread it around me, and start inquiring about our guests by the lobby. I exchange small talk and pleasantries with the regulars then head to the Kimball grand piano. The requests in classical music are threatening to bring my mind to a rancid state. I keep reminding myself of the money I make here, which allows me to rent Mama's studio in the first place.

It's hard to focus this evening. I imagine performing somewhere else, something else, instead of selling my proficient playing. Nothing in my performance is genuine right now. All of it is mechanical. I understand that. I accept it. I need the money, and this place gives good money, great tips and excellent exposure. All what new New York loves crosses these doors. The first element to greet them is their idea of New York personified:

'Even the lobby has a cultured piano player in an expensive suit! He reminds me of my boss or some big shot from back where or back when, but who is at 'my' service! Mine! Here, let me throw him some bucks and make him play my song! My, my he does look expensive, and that fishbowl of tips holds Franklins. I can do this. I am a guest here and it means I can compare to the folks around. I will belong. Here is another hefty bill my bald friend. Be a good sport and play some black jazz.'

Nothing to make a tacky lobby look more refined than banking on the few service people you choose to keep at the entrance, as well as their attire and accessories. None of us minds playing in the deceitful idea either. We know we are selling the dream to foreigners and Midwesterners. If we sell it correctly, generous tips are the least of the perks.

Past four in the morning, while I hear the noises of life from the apartments surrounding ours, I go through a mental check. I play on my phalanxes to a familiar sensation, and the beats soon follow a pattern. I know I'm onto something. I spend the next hours on my Moog in the living room, where we keep the instruments and practice. I'm exhausted, and elated by the new sounds. By dawn, I choose to go on a walk while building up the melodies further in my mind. I can hear the final pieces and their delicate and overpowering turns. Only a little more and I could afford the Greenwich studio for few hours again, and bring the tracks to optimal structure.

A Folie in New York

I spend the whole day sleeping. I had canceled some plans with an old friend group. But come eight at night, I show up at the bar to their pleasant surprise, and get a loud welcome. They know they wouldn't have had the best of time without the soul of the party. We speak the same language after all, and I happen to have an edge when it comes to banking on my hyphenated identity. It's not too tricky to navigate being at night with the folks of the morning, especially when it's this particular bunch, delightful people with a refreshing naivety and rough manners. We talk about women and European politics. We head to the local discotheque and dance. We curse our luck with women, and have American beer that has no savoir-vivre. I slip away with a drunk girl who is handsy. She doesn't care about where we are until I leave her in the cab and exit by the old industrial street. I changed my mind sweetheart, but thank you for the ride. She is too drunk to do much about it anyway.

There is light near the door of the bookstore building. I become alert and tread carefully, but it's Mo doodling in his notebook, a flashlight in his mouth. He doesn't react to my presence. I sigh and whisper:

"You freaked me out."

"Sorry."

He stands and interrupts a gesture. I open the door and let us in. I wonder whether he comes every day and how long he waits. But I stop asking myself such questions. That's his problem, not mine. We quickly get into the dance. Mo is more practical about it, as if he got into a routine. I, on the other hand, keep a certain distance. My mind is still analyzing in parallel.

When he initiates, I ask him.

"You're using protection out there?"

He nods with insistence, impatient to get back. I hold his face in my hand and insist.

"Look at me, what are you using?"

"Condoms."

"You should start getting tested. There is a clinic by West Chelsea, discrete and efficient. I will give you the address."

"Ok..."

I keep him at bay.

"No... I'm not ready... Besides... I feel like bringing a favorite touch of mine tonight. It's a celebration."

"Wha... What?"

His performance isn't a lucky strike; whoever he is practicing with or on is giving him full range.

"And I'd be more comfortable when you get yourself tested."

"I promise, you don't have to worry."

"Yet I do... And yet your words don't reassure me. So, let's go about it with a different method. Let me introduce you to other tricks in the book."

Initially, he is docile, complies, foretells the motion, and brings his force to it. Then, he becomes relentless, and every room I make is an opportunity to take over. Fair enough. I don't know when his presence became more pronounced — maybe the exertion is extra tonight — but I feel his hands everywhere, his fingers slowly pressing against my skin, and holding my head. I feel a need to pull away that I don't immediately understand, but to which I comply. In response, Mo secures me and his hands become insisting, present and forceful. Just picturing them against my thighs and my neck heightens the sensual impact, and intoxicates me. I'm losing control without planning for it, and I'm not sure whether I want that. Maybe he will take the opportunity to push beyond my limits? I try to get a hold of myself, but Mo's hands are on me again, claws traveling around. I can't stop thinking about them, and I'm provoked to furry.

When he is done, he is not really. He secures me against him while catching his breath in my neck. His hands close on mine, and sure enough, all I want is to bring them to my mouth, cover them with my lips and push them against my cheek.

"Josef?"

"…"

"I didn't get my fill yet."

Then get tested…

I can't answer out loud. My mind is still busy navigating the burst of lust still reverberating through my flesh, way after the deed is done. Fuck you, Mo. I promise I will fuck you so raw, the outbursts will pursue you well into the daylight life. For now, I'm scattered. I'm fractured, and I need to piece myself together, just later, maybe wait some more. I think it's the optimal state. I fear being a whole entity right now: It would mean withstanding this intensity and being in this heightened condition. And I don't know what would come out of it.

"I practice too, Josef."

He pushes his hands against my mouth, exposing my secret desires. He pushes my mouth open and I close my eyes.

"Maybe I'm not like you, but I'm learning as well."

His other hand reaches down, putting me in a lock as he whispers.

"You can be the puppy now if you want."

What a bastard. I smile and turn. I face him with a sudden wakefulness.

"You think you learned it all, didn't you?"

He is quiet, assessing me back.

"No one knows it all, not even you."

"I don't pretend to. But I know enough to no longer play innocent, or appeal to those who seek such underdeveloped little things like puppies. Worse yet, they can't plead innocence, they choose ignorance. Ignorance on purpose. I know enough to know the boundaries of my territory, when to expand it and what to attempt. And you, my friend, are getting cocky. I'm guessing this is the rowdy phase of puppyhood. What's next, will you be urinating on my own piss?"

"I told you it's an insult. I don't take being a dog as a compliment."

I scoff and turn to the side.

"Let's get some sleep and not spoil the night."

He heads to the bathroom and comes back while I'm still putting myself back together. Behind the safety of closed eyes, I am surprised and wary at the fact that I almost lost it. I am not going to sleep right now. I'm going to wonder whether this may happen again. It's time to let this one loose for good then.

"Mo...?"

"What?"

"Why don't you like being called a dog when you seem to behave like one?"

"Do you mock me now? Disrespect me?"

"How often are you by this place? How long do you wait for me? You have your own 'gusto' now. So why do you bother coming back?"

He is quiet.

"If you don't want to be likened to a dog, then don't behave like one."

"You don't want me to come anymore?"

"I don't care. As long as you don't make a fuss over who I am, how I conduct business and who I fuck, you are free to do whatever you want with your downtime, including loyally lurking around the place where your first fuck took place."

He turns to his side, and is quiet. I work on my breathing and leave him be for now.

In the morning, there is a chance Mo is rushing away from me. Instead, when we get to the ground floor, he slowly corners me, reaches out to my lips and into my pants, then reminds me of his touch and his warmth. I don't return the favor, and it puts me in an ill mood. I really need to get rid of this one. He doesn't seem to care when I move forward. He kisses me before looking at the door, then asks:

"Would you like to grab breakfast?"

"Breakfast?"

"Somewhere else. Not the diner?"

I assess him and he is nervous. I need to say no.

"Only if you're buying."

"I don't know if it's a place where I can do that."

I nod. Maybe it's for the better. We both head out to the bus station. Mo takes a key out and unlocks a red Volvo. He opens the passenger door next to him and invites me in. The outside is clean and average, but the inside is quality leather. He has a working stereo and a cup holder. The seats behind are covered with papers, books and little mockups. What looked like a briefcase and pieces of wood occupied my seat. He hastily removes everything to make space for me.

"Bold choice. To have a car in New York."

"It's easier this way."

I don't want to point out it's also more expensive. I don't care. It's his life and money after all. We drive through the city, listening to the radio in silence in golden daylight. This is the moment of the day when I love riding in NYC the most, when the trash trucks finish their rounds, and the early workers are on their commute. The city then is more like the place of my youth, and not the property of corporations, tourists, and inflated fortunes. To make it now in New York is infinitely harder. It looks like the milestones are getting more challenging with time.

I keep reminding myself; more tracks, more contacts and I will certainly make it without compromising my art. Then, I too will get to live in Greenwich Village. I too will lead this pathetic existence with at least some degrees of freedom. I picture myself able to afford privacy, trust and care, free to lead my life behind the scenes, however I want, confident in a place I could call home, and secure in my art. I know it will be conditioned freedom, but if I can hold a hand by a breakfast table in an open space without worrying about anything, that would be an achievement on its own. Even if it's a private patio or a fenced garden, even if it's not ideal with that person, I wouldn't care. It would be one major win to take, significant enough that it's a main goal in my life. Thinking of a Love Alcove being next to the room where I make music is my personal kind of high, and still gives me the drive to keep it together, increase my patience and be true to a regal persona amidst the chaos of this absurd world.

"You must know by now I like your hands. It doesn't grant you any more power on me than the one I grant you willingly, though."

"I wasn't sure at first. It's the weirdest thing to me... But thanks for the free confirmation."

"Keep in mind the rest of what I said."

"Yes."

"I don't mind relinquishing control on my own terms and being the one to grant power... Again, on my own terms... But don't make the rookie mistake of thinking you are taking it for yourself."

"Of all the things we could talk about, of all the things you could tell me, you choose to tell me this?"

"Do I hear frustration?"

"No, just curiosity. Of all the things you could tell me or discuss with me, you choose to let me know that you didn't lose control yesterday, but you granted it."

"I didn't say that. And yes, for someone who is learning, I think it's important to know. The illusion of power you're holding is what grants power over you."

"What makes you think I approach our physical relationship from that stand?"

"Then what was yesterday about?"

"It was about finding other ways to please you, when you clearly don't want to be pleased."

I chuckle. Mo insists:

"I don't mean it like that. Let me clarify. You want the sensations, but on your own terms, and this by default diminishes the range of pleasure to which you could have access."

"So, if I tell you I like coffee and you serve me coffee few times, you think you're entitled to forcefully pouring juice down my throat? To broaden my palate?"

He opens his mouth, then keeps quiet. I slowly shake my head and smile.

"I'm telling you, Mo: I am not a know-it-all. I know enough though. Especially when it comes to me. I've been around. I've sampled enough. What did you do in the meantime? How is your palate? Could you tell me what do you prefer and why? Look at you being an active homosexual... For six months now? And already deciding what I like and don't like."

I see him wince. He is about to say something, but wisely keeps quiet. If he pulls the 'I'm not a faggot' card,

I'd have the best excuse to send him packing. Actually, this is a good idea.

"Speaking of which, how long have you known?"

"Known what?"

"That you are a raging gay homosexual."

"Maybe... Maybe when I was a kid?"

"How?"

"I realized I liked playing with myself more than playing with girls. And I wanted something like mine to play with."

I laugh at his answer. He scrutinizes my face with pronounced nervousness:

"You and me and every man in this world, Mo. You, me and every man in this world."

"How about you?"

"When I opened my eyes to sex, and found out it only equated to pleasure when it's a phallic vision... What are you planning to do with your life?"

"What do you mean?"

"As a raging gay homosexual that is?"

"I... It's too early to decide. I haven't made up my mind on what I want."

"There is time for that, as long as you make efficient use of it... And spread your wings."

"I know what I don't want, though."

"Good start."

"I don't want to be like you."

I scoff, and reply with an equally low blow:

"It takes a hearty serving of intelligence and patience, so you are safe..."

I think about it a little, and can't help but add:

"Besides, you were lucky I was your first. That takes you off that path already, believe me."

We assess each other, and decide to leave it at that. We get to Manhattan, drive through a neat neighborhood close to Riverside Drive and Upper West Side. It's a part of town I vaguely know from the news, but haven't been through. The streets have a powerful presence yet are eerily empty, as if the tall buildings were inhabited by ghosts. By one of them, Mo honks twice. A doorman comes rushing and opens the garage. They briefly salute each other, and he gets inside.

"I'm assuming this is the part where you try some monkey business."

It was a half-joke. Mo shakes his head and says:

"You're the New Yorker, not me."

I repress a smirk as we get out of the car and into the building. The elevator is not working so we are taking a narrow corridor towards the hallway. The doorman is extra in his manners. Despite the hour and the odd assistance he provided, his smile is wide. He greets us with pleasantries, asking whether he could be of service; laundry to be taken care of, shopping, bills... Mo awkwardly dismisses his talk and paces inside. I'm sure he must be paying him generously. Just how filthy rich is this puppy?

"It's upstairs."

The building must have known better days, but its chic shabbiness is intact. If I didn't know any better, I would assume it to be a large townhouse or some sort of hotel.

"What's this place?"

"Some old apartment hotel building that was evacuated during renovations. It will be destroyed at some point. But for now, I can live here without hassle. Electricity and water are running in my place."

We reach the highest floor, go through a corridor with an art deco mangy carpet, and walk towards an unnumbered door at the end. The first space is an empty and large living room. It appears to be a duplex with two elevated sections facing one another. The kitchen in the middle is by far the most crowded area with machines, groceries and trash bags. The tall windows have been clumsily covered by ill-fitted white curtains and glued newspapers. Both sides looked over the quiet streets and the other rows of buildings. I hear pigeons and spot the desks and mockups behind the stairs to our right, and the improvised living room with the solitary couch and big coffee table on the left. Mo quickly throws his coat by the stairs leading to the first floor of the duplex, then heads to the kitchen.

"Coffee and eggs?"

I nod and notice the coffee machine. Mo has everything, from the outsourced beans to the Bosch grinder, the automatic espresso machine and the optional milk steamer. I take care of the coffee while he prepares the scrambled eggs. We sit by a granite counter on bar stools. The exquisite aroma of high-quality beans mingling with the fragrant and seasoned eggs put me in a good mood. This moment is some serious coinage, and requires serious coinage to appreciate it as well.

"What did you put on my eggs?"

"You don't know?"

I smell and can't tell.

"No."

"How about you give it a try?"

"I may not like it. You should have asked beforehand."

"If you don't like it, I'll make more. There are plenty of eggs in the fridge."

I try it. I find the combination surprising flavorful. The spice is an epiphany.

"So, what is it?"

"Freshly ground cumin."

I vaguely associate it with Indian curries, which I don't favor that much. I'm surprised by the delicious and new flavor the spice gives to the eggs though.

"Cumin and salt. You like it?"

I smile and say:

"Better than the greasy spoon. The coffee is optimal."

"Bon Appetit."

I turn and examine the covered windows while enjoying the coffee.

"If you need privacy, I'm sure you could afford better curtains than whatever you improvised here..."

He points upstairs, where I can discern the frame of a gray bed and some closets.

"The duplex is private enough. I just can't stand those buildings."

"How ironic."

"It's tacky. It's shabby and has no sense of cohesion to it."

Mo shrugs, then adds:

"New York City is basically a sloppy puzzle, made of wacky pieces from different other puzzles... No one bothers putting in any effort to harmonize them. If anything, it's only self-coercion which keeps it together."

"Yet, if it wasn't for that heterogeneous aspect, you wouldn't have found any sort of freedom here. Perhaps you should sojourn in the Bible Belt and get some perspective."

"I don't mean to trash your city... I came to this place with intent. I came here to... To be free. To live my life on my own terms, and find room to experiment with my craftsmanship. I'm not about to waste that opportunity."

"I think it's no longer the point. Maybe it's time to find opportunities that only this place has to offer, and make use of them."

I take a walk in the open space and examine the old mockups gathering dust by the floor. I reason that what Mo works on currently is on the desks, the clean and carefully put together blocks. I examine those buildings, and can't help but notice the diligence and delicate sensitivity gone into making the shapes and decorating the walls. It looked familiar, but I couldn't pinpoint it.

"Josef..."

I had hoped Mo was the square type of architect, that he was the sort who followed the pseudo-artist path where no one is really an artist, and most copy what the client and/or the environment conditioned them to pursue. I really need to stop this one from coming around.

"Josef..."

I can't focus on one idea at the time, for one building's shape and its general air bother me. There is something to them which feels familiar, and it bothers me that I can't pinpoint it. Does it have to do with buildings from New York? It must be it. There must be a subconscious template I'm finding in here, though my gut tells me otherwise. And why is it stirring discomfort in me?

"Josef..."

"What is it Mo, I'm listening..."

Mo comes close:

"What is that?"

"Some crappy ideas..."

"What are you trying to achieve?"

"I can't even convey it in shapes so far, let alone in words... I was hoping American education would help on that. I guess it's like my professor says, I just have to be patient and let it come out of me when it's ready."

He wants to talk about something else, but I insist:

"Why don't you try to articulate it then?"

"Do you know anything about architecture?"

"Not really, but I know how to articulate music synthesis to someone who didn't study music... So, why don't you give it a try... Humor me if you need to."

"What does it matter now?"

I take a cheap and needless shot. Effective in getting something out of someone who thinks of themselves as a creative. The words may change but the bottom line stays the same. I know it and I'm sure Mo knows it too, at least on some level.

"Because this reminds me of Brownsville in Brooklyn, NYC. And I'm not sure you would have ventured on such side of town, at least not on your own, and enough to get all these uncanny details. Were you inspired by academic references or benchmarks models at NYU?"

"This has nothing to do with New York! This is my own style and I highly doubt it would be on such... sloppy streets."

"And yet..."

"No one tried to rally such concepts. I myself am still struggling to do so... I couldn't find anybody who could help so far either, let alone have attempted something similar."

At my unconvinced silence, he nervously points out at the doors of an isolated and sophisticated laced construction.

"I'm trying to find a potential intersection between brutalist and Moorish architecture. This Folie was the starting idea and it went somewhere. The gates are a bit much, and the main building is... Structurally unstable. Looks like the undigested vomit of a novice. I can't rally the naked prismatic features to the organic flow of the Moorish tendencies without suffocating the brutalism, or falling into some psychedelic futurism, and I absolutely hate that."

The imposing and forceful reliefs of long gray constructions come to my mind, dwarfing the figures, who are already puny and crushed. There is hidden grief, hidden harshness to an already oppressive austerity. My grandparents keep a distance and a solemnity. My mother doesn't smile. I only ever knew her as a jolly human being, and those pictures of her youth were a slap to the face. There was a time I couldn't fathom her, or anyone else living in such places. It broke the heart of a child who couldn't articulate his melancholy.

I get a hold of myself. This is the worst time to dive into the memories and a radical pool of old feelings. I don't know what to say except manipulate what seemed like a door of the hexagonal construction. The finely sculpted papers with the arabesque forms opened up to show the empty hexagonal interior, save for fine linen stripes glued to the top, reminding me of the Love Alcove's ones.

I wince at the realization: It rallies the intimacy and simple taste of my carnal sanctuary to the penultimate display of wealth; real estate for no purpose at all, save perhaps its artistic value to the connoisseurs. And perhaps few curtains reminiscent of 'a phase', of a life reduced to mere memories. Are you already there, New York? Will you forsake us and make way to such notions within your bosom? As time goes by, I hope for a better future, and I see the betterment of many prospects. Will it be worth it if by the end, New York of my memories is no longer there to witness my fulfilled desires? When I could finally live life on my terms, just not within the boroughs and streets I had always pictured?

"You know what, Josef... It's like you said. This place is rich with opportunities. I have the means to figure things out... Besides, they allow such tacky aesthetics everywhere, there is no place sacred enough... So, I think I will get a shot here at exercising my own art, and get it right before bestowing it on a rightful and worthy place."

I repress a scowl. I stare at him, wondering whether he understood what he said, and whether we are still talking about piled up concrete at this point. His focus and intent are heavy on me.

"Josef..."

"Spit it out already."

"Josef... I know what you may think of doing... Of ending things..."

I have to detach my attention from the sight of the other desks filled with his architectural models, and possibly future defiling monuments to this city. I have to focus.

"What of it?"

"I understand you might have some second thoughts for God knows what reasons..."

"It's simple. I don't do fuck buddies."

"Really?"

I don't need to justify myself.

"But I haven't had my fill yet..."

"Too bad... Many of us don't. Closure is a luxury, not a right."

"Then let's try this.... Stay with me here. Let me take it out of my system since you don't care... It's a discrete place, it's close to transportation. I have everything we may need, and if there is anything else, we could figure it out..."

This is a tricky offer. I don't care. So far, I don't. But I can't lie to myself: There is a danger zone, there is a possibility to fall there. I can't narrow on the point where it would happen. What if I admit to it and end it all? The self-destructive inclination resurfaces and wonders about the other option: Giving in, enjoying the ride to the fullest and dealing with the crash later. The moment this delicious thought pops up, a vicious whip brings back my sang-froid. I answer without the need to think about an answer:

"What would be next? We have breakfast together every morning? We fuck in daylight? A domesticated partner for your own delights... Then what? We settle into habits and intimate routines in the privacy of walls, but show up to parties with girls? I start listening? I start talking even? You tell me about here and there? A domesticated ménage à deux? We bicker? We play mind games? We fuck? We even make love?"

I scoff at my words, then add, shacking my head:

"Reality hasn't hit you yet Mo, has it? At this point, what would it take for you to understand? Holding hands in public so that the idea of New York disappears and the reality of it hits you in all sorts of ways? What will you tell your folks when you are bruised with broken ribs, Mo? Or when your deer eyes get gauged as a collateral? Or when they ask for kids? Tsk, tsk, tsk... What freedom you have here, you are already using it. Whatever that head of yours sings, on the other hand, is some fairyland that doesn't exist. And if you want to make it exist, be my guest. But I'm not about to be one of its residents."

I pace towards the door. He holds my hand, and shoves a key in my palm.

"Please... In case..."

Outside, my steps are wide and erratic. I quickly put as much distance from the apartment as possible. A mix of anger and resentment that are all too familiar threaten to overwhelm me. It's useless, don't go down this path, Josef.

Times like these remind me why my peers don't like this lot of prey, the clueless linear ones, and dealing with them. We don't even speak the same language at some point. Every word a versed gay would use comes with its burdening history, and is uttered carefully in matters of intimacy and private life. But these idiots still use the heteronormative vocabulary thinking they are entitled to the same rituals, and the images they grew up with. Just take the figure of Jacky or Audrey out and put theirs instead, and it should work with the right guy. It's not the right guy or the right country — those are problems of tax brackets —, it's the right world.

Times like these when I falter or start losing it get sparse. But when they happen, it's a burning reminder. I'm still at an elastic phase, though; I know that once I calm down, dive into daylight's own troubles and meditate the situation, I will quickly be back to normal. I keep the key with the rest of the keys I have. There is a difference: Mo's key is black and slick. It comes with its own keychain: A scorpion trapped in resin. I scowl at the creature then smirk. Of course, he would have something like this as some sort of sigil. This must be him in the daylight too, when he is out in the streets, at his classes with his peers or with his family. It doesn't matter whether it's an innocent act or something of meaning. It could have been a cobra too, and I would asphyxiate it in my pocket. I wouldn't take the same liberties with this animal. The structure of its unspoken rules is erratic. I keep it in my pocket though and head to work.

Summer in Black Curtains

The heat drives New Yorkers to walk outside and seek bars with terraces. It's the perfect season for outdoor concerts. Though we find different venues, we don't get booked again in most. The Techno audience is unsure and stiff, when they are not openly discourteous. The guys agree the brightened outdoor is not our scene, and I agree with them. But I need the Moog to get some air, to see the light a little bit. I keep thinking it will bring up inspiration or music which would connect with more people. This is a slow process, and in my patience, I am bothered by the heat. It bothers me too during my nocturnal activities: The Love Alcove doesn't have a cooling unit, and there is so much a fan could do. Therefore, my carnal dances take place in other rooms, with less than few regulars since many have escaped NYC for the summer, or at the apartment of a stranger, which I generally avoid if I can. The idea of the Love Alcove is heavy though; I blame the weather and my unwillingness to face the possibility of Mo's presence.

I think of calling my mother and I know it's not a good idea. I never call her at night. I never call her without a good reason. We have our monthly strolls through Central Park to talk and catch up. She is entertaining and funny. I know I get it from her. I also know if I call her now, being chatty would be the least of her concerns. She will know something is off and won't rest afterwards. No, maybe I should have gone with friends on that trip to Long Island, relaxed for some time. But I'm not safe there. It's too out in the open and anybody could see us. Anybody could talk. Word travels. My night life could be exposed to the daylight.

Most importantly, summer is when opportunities flow, and the music industry is no exception. I need to wrap up the albums. Therefore, I need to play and earn money to afford the Greenwich studio. It's becoming a more challenging quest. I used to be able to make money easily, but it's getting stuffier to do so on the spot. Everyone wants to pay later, try you first, see credentials, ask the references. It's no longer 'there you go, honest work, and there is your honest money'. New York is pushing its residents to prostitute themselves for less, which is thrown their way later.

I lose some of my patience. I do cave in and reach out to my Alma Mater. I get few gigs covering up for a pianist on vacation. I accompany a jazz band. It's good pay, but I hear my soul aching inside my bones. At every concert and encore, at every accolade and afterparty, I keep a smiling face and a talkative well-rounded mood. Underneath, I'm nursing the frustration and the feeling that I'm selling out in a disgusting way. Would it be selling out if it's for the sake of my own music? No, there is more to it. I'm selling out a part of me to another hideous and forbidden part of me.

There is nothing to fear. I need to remind myself I'm not the centerpiece. I need to act accordingly. I'm just the accompanying sound, the support. It takes off the heat and makes me a more amiable piano player. I will gladly spend time speaking of the star of the show rather than my technique, the performance of other musicians and the beauty of the musical conversation they bring to life. Part of it may be true, but the zealous compliments are byproducts of my wish to be forgotten on that scene, or to be remembered as someone who did jazz before finding their true vocation, alternative synthetic music. That sounds good enough in my head. The silver lining is I get to meet many people from the music industry, some who came to be good friends and reliable contacts. It's just that their interest is restricted to what makes money and/or brings in the patronage of the old stuffy fortunes. Neither of which particularly applies to synthetic wave music.

After few one-night stands which were as bland and necessary as showers after long sweaty days, I delight in finding out that a regular of mine is back in town. We meet at a hotel room for business. He is all there, yet it doesn't feel the same. I am applied and push beyond my usual boundaries and regular performances to compensate. I know he notices. We are used to each other enough at this point. He doesn't ask, but he takes over and tries to roughly control the carnal dance, and bring me back to my own flesh. Though I like his brand of provocation, it's a little too rough to my taste, and I don't wish for it to last long. It would bring up further negativity to the bed, mainly angered tension or something sickening. At the same time, I have trouble articulating it in an alluring fashion so that my host doesn't get offended, and doesn't get an idea of what's truly going on either.

"I'm afraid I'm not bringing the art to 'the sexcapade' today. I'm sorry..."

He finishes and rolls next to me, quizzical.

"You called me..."

"I am very happy to see you. He is very happy to see you too. Haven't you noticed?"

"Are you alright?"

"I don't know man... Maybe it's just..."

But he doesn't care. He doesn't want an answer. I know that. This is why we are in this together in the first place. I wrap up by crudely offering a blowjob. We effectively end the business meeting, one of us at least climaxing enough.

"I think you're stressed. Here is a crazy idea: You should have sex to relax."

I smile at his joke while he cleans up and gets ready to leave.

"I will make it up to you, next time."

"You'd better. You're my favorite after all. And I don't turn down a private dinner party at the mayor's house for banal business meetings."

"I promise you. Next time, I will make you scream his name if you want."

He leaves. I spend long minutes under the shower, trying to even my breathing, then recompose my thinking. Something is shaky and I know. I know. Sexual performance is something I have always been sure I wouldn't lose. That fact alone had been affirming in many ways to me. Now, I am having trouble performing in that area. It's not a bad night or a passable one. It's something frustrating happening because of some blockage somewhere. I shave closely and make sure I'm smooth everywhere. I wear an outfit that turns me on just by looking at myself. I'm off on a spontaneous hunt. I know I'm not in the optimal mood, but I will be extra-careful.

I closely circle strangers. I'm more ruthless than the usual, but it saves me time. They aren't open about their testing or they try to lie. I stick one in the bathroom of a mainstream nightclub and keep the interaction away from my body, both of us trying to ferociously rid each other of their lust. I sit down and even my breath. The sounds of American pop and the dancing crowd finally echo in my head. What am I doing? And here? What the fuck am I doing? I look at my hands, still dirty. Do I not like my own hands? What would I do without them? I'd be lost. I'd be completely lost.

I pour soap and energetically clean them, suddenly aware of my unstable state. I head to the Harlem apartment, and find a stranger passed out on my own bed. Nevermind. I grab my Moog and head to the old industrial street. My heartbeats become slower as I come close to the Love Alcove. I become calmness incarnated when I see no one. I go through the foreign section row then head to the Love Alcove. I clean up then plug my instrument. It keeps me company for the night, comforts me in my loneliness and shields me from bad decisions, repressed memories, and destructive yearnings.

I don't know why I cry at times. I black out on the sounds I'm making, but I sense something is coming together. I keep recording the parts. When my instrument exhausts its possibilities, I mix them in my head. What would I not give to have my own studio, to be able to go there at any hour of the day, and turn my frustrations and well of pain into a colorful parade of all impossible objects: Offspring of fridges and gates, China dolls who are disciples to crickets and roaches, creatures who created empty vessels to masquerade as living humans, the spawn of shepherds who had fucked each other to their fill, and all the foreign books about raising bees of clays, and waltzing garbagemen on mine riddled territories.

When will I finally get to a place where I could sublimate the excess into art, at every ungodly hour? Let the voracious will to live as I see fit take every fucking turn it wants?

At the late hours of the night, the door opens. I don't have time to react. I'm absorbed with my instrument, and never had an intruder before. My stillness and performance go uninterrupted as I lack the reaction time at that point. I can't process the presence or the stab of fear. He comes closer. I register eventually that it's Mo. He looks at my instrument in bewilderment. I have trouble speaking, so I just keep playing and replaying the same part, committing it to memory and recording. He sits next to me on the bed, waits for me to finish, his hands visible and distracting. Once I'm done, my throat is rough, as if I haven't spoken in a long time. He extracts a paper and I recognize the format. He holds it for a bit and the fear comes back. I don't know whether it's for myself or him. I almost snatch it and go through the lines fast; it was clear, and it dated from a week ago.

"You never came around. I had to do this shit every week."

He scoffs and says:

"They must think I'm a nutjob down at that clinic. But I know you wouldn't want a paper from a month ago, and you wouldn't believe me if I told you I was careful, and nothing was happening anyway."

No. Don't be gentle. Don't be considerate. Don't take my requests into consideration. Not like that.

"I came here once in a while, but you never showed up, not anymore... This place is hot."

Don't come here anymore. Leave.

I exhale and ask:

"How did you get inside?"

"I forced the door. I'm sorry."

"Now every nutjob can get in?"

"Can we fix it? Discreetly?"

"I will see to it, but you will pay..."

"Of course..."

I put the Moog aside and look at the bed.

"I'm tired and I want to sleep."

"Why don't you come and sleep over? It's so hot in here. My place has good AC... And you can take a shower. Josef, you stink."

I have no strength in me to fight. I physically can't get my mouth to utter words, to send Mo away. I stand slowly and pack. He wants to grab my instrument, but I resist.

"Don't worry. I will be very careful."

And he is. He doesn't take it like a piece of fragile equipment. He handles it like a newborn, and steps silently so that it doesn't wake up. In no time, we are in his car, then in his apartment. The day and the restless nights are catching up with me. I take a hot and long shower until my muscles are completely relaxed. I check on my Moog; it's on a table near the rest of the desks. I go upstairs and slowly extend my aching body on the bed. I let a moan of satisfaction, and pass out without delay. I vaguely sense the presence of Mo next to me, sound asleep as well.

I don't immediately wake up. Instead, I wait for the alarm or for the sun. Neither comes, so by the time I get up, it's past midday on the clock next to Mo. I don't have any pressing affairs, but I haven't slept that late in months. Consequently, a thumper is knocking against my forehead. Mo is next to me, asleep. I take care of myself in the bathroom, then come back to sit next to him. He groans.

"Josef, are you awake already?"

"Yes."

He groans again.

"I need some coffee, or this headache will blow up."

"You know where everything is..."

I move in the darkened apartment while trying to make out the weather outside. Mo wasn't bluffing; It is cool in his place. He had also set up new and dark curtains which hid the windows and the morning. Only the yellow lamps of the downstairs area provide some semblance of light. The apartment was trapped in a sunset without a sun, and conveyed a morbidly beautiful intimacy. I refuse to use my head right now. I want to take in the moment as it is without thinking beyond it. I make coffee under the yellow light of the counter and pour myself a cup.

"Do you like the curtains?"

I nod and resume drinking. Mo comes down and I state:

"You're a pertinacious man, aren't you?"

"I don't know what that means."

"Incessant... Persistent."

He shrugs and says without much thought:

"I don't really know someone who isn't. I used to think it was part of the requirements to lead a decent life. I came here and it's all different. It could be liberating in many ways though."

I assess him and stay silent. His lustful stare is obvious though his tone of voice doesn't match it.

"Are you still tired? You can go back to sleep if you want..."

"I have plenty to do."

He stares at the Moog and I nod.

"You can plug it here. I won't mind. I have some archiving to do myself."

He presses his lips against my neck, my cheek then my mouth. Their warmth and insistence speak of his desire. I do my best not to answer to his touch. At least, he is keeping his hands away. I breathe deeply to maintain my composure and he lets go.

"I will not bother you, I promise."

Mo heads to an inclined table with a cup of coffee. He turns on the lamp by his side, drags a stool and takes out his notebook. He checks a page and resumes tracing on the large paper. What a bastard.

My mind is not clear enough. I need to get hold of myself. I need to clean myself. I take the opportunity of a hot shower to clear my mind, cease the movement and quiet the cacophony threatening to take over my body and emotions. Navigating lust with a fragile vessel is useless. Just quiet down the voice and let go. When I switch to cold water, I'm suddenly back. I'm inhabiting my flesh, my own flesh, my territory. It is mine. It is mine, and I inhabit it completely. The goosebumps fade. My fingers are fully dilated, and I see them. Freshness is instilled underneath my skin.

Going out of the shower is odd. The darkness wrapping the living room is uncanny. I'm not used to it in houses, or during the daylight time. Darkness in here acts as a time suspender. Perhaps that's what I need right now after all. I go down the stairs. Mo smiles at me:

"All good?"

"I will make... 'noise'."

"We're the only ones here. No one will complain."

A whole building of multiple apartments and no one lives in it save Mo. Electricity and water are running too. I abstain from asking questions and grab my Moog. I drag a table by the closest plug and set up shop. My decision-making is clear though the lustful choices and scenarios bubble underneath. I make it succinct and transactional to myself: This place offers great acoustics and good accommodation. I may be able to wrap the rest of the tracks before the end of the summer. No, I will be making inquiries for potential label companies before the end of summer. I will book the Greenwich studio, do my audio engineering, and have the albums ready. Then, the creative process won't be rushed anymore. I won't have to make my art suffer my impatience, and I will have a plethora of choices to offer. I will have better prospects.

The thoughts take time to align but eventually, my mind is back to serving the current goal: Assemble melodies and finalize the tracks. I toil on my instrument undisturbed. I feel Mo's presence. I sense him come and go. He states he is grabbing some sandwiches for both of us. When my hotel shift is about to start, I finally stop and reach for the sandwich and more coffee. He stares at me with anticipation and I look at my Moog.

"I'll be leaving for the evening."

"You don't have to leave."

"I will be leaving, though..."

Will he dare ask or just assume? He nods, not surprised and not happy.

"Then, would you come back? Whenever you are done..."

I am still not packing my apparatus yet. I was wondering whether I would. I had made significant progress today. It is undeniably a good conducive environment for my work. But then again, the bar is pretty low in that regard.

"I will."

"You still have the key?"

"I do."

"Do you want a change of clothes? I think you can fit in mine."

"I don't know if you have something appropriate in your wardrobe."

"Check it out."

Not only does the bastard have a set of elegant suits and assorted ties, but out of the bunch, only two were labels. The rest is custom-made and uniquely crafted.

"Are you fine with me borrowing any?"

"Yes, please... I barely wear that stuff anyway. You can keep it for all I care."

To not care, to willingly give such expensive statements... No wonder the rookie has a distorted view and unconscious vulnerability. He must have a fair lot of privilege to his name. I swiftly get dressed and stare at my Moog for a moment; I don't think I ever left it in anybody's care before. My roommates have always been serious musicians and band members. No one had to spell out the care and respect an instrument should get. Mo guesses my thoughts, and states:

"You have my word. My word, Josef. Nothing will happen to your machine... You look very handsome by the way."

"It's the fabric quality and the adjusted measures... Money makes anything beautiful."

He scoffs, but doesn't object. There is tension in the air. I'm not giving into this, especially right now. I head out and ask the doorman about the directions for downtown Manhattan. He generously helps me figure out the lines. I thank him and he warmly smiles at me, thanking me back.

Ménage à Deux

At the tacky lobby, a drunk customer comes at me, now and then, to make far-fetched requests. He doesn't seem to know the difference between a piano piece, a violin one or a symphonic composition. Music has to be one of the most paradoxical art forms to consume: People think they can listen to hundreds of records and do armchair appreciation and recommendations, when the blatant language in itself betrays the actual understanding. I smile through it though, and foresee the melodies they are able to identify. I butcher the piece for the benefit of the chorus, and improvise some theme which stitches it together with whatever comes next. And they love it. And they tip. They tip well.

Another one, more reserved yet equally drunk, slips his business card with his number and a plus next to a woman's name. She has his last name. The rest is up to me. Another pays the lobby boy so that he moves the chairs to face me. I zero in on him and remember him from few months ago: He came here to visit an ailing relative. I remember his accents and manners, the conversation details, and tones. I narrow it quickly to the Catholic background. I dynamically transition the performance to something more melancholic, a personal take on 'Ave Mundis Spes Maria'. I grant him few minutes, and get served a drink. This often happens, especially on crowded nights. The bartender knows to get me the same drink than the client but dilute it with water.

Tonight is a great night for tips. The fishbowl by the table near me is filling up with some generous bills. Regulars and familiar faces are showing up. The lobby and bar are getting crowded. A chic looking woman has been talking to whoever listens about her piano skills. I ask her to join me and accompany her, providing a mellow performance with my left play to damp potentially false notes and bring up her colorful execution. She plays well but slow, and stumbles on few difficult notes. She did study piano after all. I raise my glass to her. I clock her perfume with vanilla undertone when she leans over and slips a key to her room. It's that effortless when you have money, even for a woman. It comes with the territory. I don't begrudge this fact. She secured a space where she is sovereign. But that perfume is a crime: If I were to sleep with a woman, I'd need someone whose smell is as rich as their age. The prepubescent perfumes are icky on anyone. I don't need them to be on a woman on top of that to utterly rebuff her attempt.

It doesn't help either that at some point, someone tips and requests 'happy jazz'. My patience was already running thin from playing classical music of other men. Had I been a full-timer here, I would have been alienated in no time from answering the same mainstream requests over and over and over again.

Luke, the night shift manager, would sure love to see me here full time. He knows I retain the crowd. He loves my attitude. He says he would increase my wages, get me benefits. And I would almost think of giving in, were it not for the experience itself: Going through the motion reminds me why I want to flay my skin by the end of such long nights, and why I expand efforts towards socializing and turning a crowd of strangers into acquaintances who know one another. It is nothing but a coping mechanism against the monotony of the piano and the music choices. So much that by the end of the night, yes everyone has made good money, and yes I leave with the blessings of the staff and the smiles of the few fans who want to know when I'm playing next, where and whether I would play at their weddings or teach their relatives. But inside, gray mush has coated me, and I need time and effort to unwind. It's a self-inflicted rancid violation, and I don't know many things to alleviate it.

All I know is that I am grateful I won't have to do it again the following day. I shudder at the thought of this miasmic bath being a daily ritual. I doubt my compartmentalization, my self-awareness and sense of control would shield me long and deep enough. With time, I will forget it's gray mush coating, and I will come to believe it's me.

Fortunately, or perhaps unfortunately, the remedy is close and potentially ready to be had. I salute the doorman and jump the stairs before reaching the apartment. I listen through the door and there is no noise. I come inside. The whole place is dark save for faint light from the first floor. I close the door as quietly as possible and head upstairs. Mo is there reading while playing with his hair. He is half-naked and relaxed under the thin sheet. He sits down once he sees me come and examines me.

"Did you have fun?"

I repress a scoff. My head is a swarm of aimless thoughts. I forgot how the initial steps of the hunt could be effective in letting them settle in their hive, leave room for the main event. I smile and say:

"I need to be in a good mood to have fun."

He doesn't understand, doesn't say anything.

"Do you want to have fun then?"

"Are we going to play Monopoly or drink while recollecting embarrassing memories?"

He is surprised. He shrugs and smiles seductively. Maybe he doesn't intend for it. It's just his smile all along.

"If you want to have fun this way, then why not? But I don't know how to play Monopoly. Is it a card game?"

I start taking off his suit and putting it neatly away before throwing the shirt in his laundry basket.

"Having sex is not exactly about having fun. Fun is the byproduct I want, not the drive for it."

"I could see that. It's... An artistic sport."

I scoff at the tacky description while I sit next to him. He could say that. I don't want to debate the statement. I reach out to his lips and he asks:

"Did you eat?"

"Don't worry, I will take care of the piping before we get into anything..."

"No, did you actually eat?"

This is an awkward question. I don't want to get into such exchanges with Mo.

"Please don't remind me of my mother in bed."

"I'm not... It's a normal question, no... Look, I thought we could have dinner. I have some spaghetti from a nice Italian restaurant. We could have dinner first then... You know."

Again with the sweet illusion of domestic life. He just doesn't register what I say. Mo takes my silence for an agreement. He goes down to the kitchen and I follow him, assessing the situation and his figure, almost with a scowl. I don't know how I feel about the arrangement anymore. Do I just let him have his little illusion? Or do I cut it short? I can't be an idiot myself and ignore the danger zone I'm flirting with right now. He grabs two big packages from the fridge and turns the stove on.

I put the packages away and secure him between my body and the table.

"Let's see how you taste first, then we can worry about your 'spaghetti'..."

"Are you sure..."

"I don't talk unless I'm certain... Now, are you ready for me?"

He doesn't hesitate and holds my neck, letting his lust answer on his behalf. I find out that I'm too hungry for his flesh, unable to coordinate my movements. I can't control my hand when it looks for his, even though the motion makes no sense, and has no harmony to the carnal dance we are partaking in. It's clumsy and ferocious. A part of me is disapprovingly witnessing the scene, but I don't care. It's like the thirsty sojourner lost in a desert. He thinks he has been having water, but it's rain droplets compared to the well of fresh pure liquid before him.

If you don't know any better, you will fall inside it, I hear that part say. I know how to climb stone walls. It's fine if I go down, it's fine I can assure you. No. This part yells that it's going to be a big problem, and loyal to its drive, as I am about to pour myself into Mo, the memories of these visceral nights of pain and drowning come to my mind. The drowning sensations from the complete and free enjoyment go hand-in-hand with the awful days of youth, the bruised neck, the bleeding body, the broken soul and the violated trust. I'm about to cry, and I understand why it is happening, and I pull back slowly while Mo is lost in the ecstasy.

He finally realizes I'm putting some distance. He aggressively reaches out to me with his hands, forcing me to stay against him. I can't help it and lift them from my body only to cover them with my lips. He says, almost begging.

"Josef... Please, let me..."

"I can't... I can't..."

"Please, please... Josef, don't..."

"I can't, it's not... I can't..."

I utter the words once more, and let go of Mo's hands with difficulty.

"You can be such a tease sometime... I..."

I don't like that word. I don't like it at all. But I can't say anything. Even if I wanted to, I doubt I could ever say anything. I manage to utter, almost in control.

"It's like that sometimes..."

He is about to speak, then he stops. I sense his frustration and I add.

"I think maybe let's eat first. I'm dizzy. Let me just..."

"Josef, is this...?"

Mo may think it's a game, a teasing sort of game. But I barely pick on his facial expressions, or posture. I can't address it right away. I need to recover from the internal whiplash. I lean against the counter and close my eyes. That's as much privacy as I can get right now. There is no motion or noise for a moment, then Mo resumes the diner preparations, albeit with a little bit more dexterity.

I understand why my head does such things. I agree. I really do. Nothing is more basic, and evident than self-preservation. But at this moment, for that one moment, I would have given anything to quiet that part of me, to forget everything altogether, and have one night for myself without any remorse or pain. It has been a long while since I've been whipped like this, and it's not because of luck, but rather for cold and calculated reasons.

Maybe I have temporarily forgotten the reasons. Maybe as people are getting uglier, it's easier to dismiss them, and harder to stumble upon potential danger zones. Besides, this is different: Nothing is at stake. I hold the power. I have control. And right now, I am more me in my own life than any other time. And the incessant thumper doesn't play jazz continuously anymore. It's different now.

I can keep telling my head this simple fact all night. I'm not about to change these granitized notions in the span of hours. It's been built so that it doesn't change on a whim. I know that because I did it. I did it to myself.

"Josef..."

Mo faces me, sitting by a stool and putting my plate next to his. He is waiting for me to sit and get my food before he starts eating. Foreign manners I suppose. He doesn't look angry, but the tension is still palpable. I wonder how it is he doesn't snap at this point. I briefly nurse the hope that he understands, and that perhaps he might have been acquainted with such inner turmoil. It's highly improbable, though. From his potential up-bringing, his actions and his manners, Mo hasn't been eaten raw by life, at least not yet. It would be too good to be true if he could understand without experiencing the pain himself. Empathy is a labor of pain and humility, and so very few openly ask for it or scour it on their own. If it's too good to be true, then it simply is. The least I could do is to not build false hopes, then take actions based on them. Dismiss them altogether. I am staring at a foreign attitude, a way of being I am not acquainted with. His people are different clay after all. I shouldn't forget that either.

I take the seat, calmer in movement and appearance, though lust runs thick underneath a fragile coat of sense. I see he doesn't make use of the Parmesan.

"This goes on top of the pasta... Like this."

I grate Parmesan he had left in the restaurant bag.

"Is that so? I was wondering what the cheese was for..."

"You've never had pasta before?"

"Yes, but there was no cheese on top. They keep asking me here to add it, but I thought it was generally some American thing. There is cheese on everything here, even on eggs and vegetables."

I smile and am about to quip, but I don't want to make fun of his culture or his eating habits. I don't feel like keeping up the momentum of the conversation either. I'm worried it would lead to a physical response.

"The first time I've had spaghetti was in a restaurant at Al-Manāmah. I accompanied my father for business there, and was allowed to pick anything on the menu. I remembered spaghetti from British cartoons and asked for it. They didn't have it, but they made it for me. It was so messy, I didn't know how to eat it. The meatballs escaped my fork. I had sauce all over me, and even stained my father's white clothes. I got a good beating after that, and wasn't allowed to order for myself for the rest of the trip."

"To be fair, it could be tricky to eat pasta when there is no guidance."

"Look at this now."

He makes optimal use of the spoon, and is clearly proud of his roll of pasta. He eats it whole with great appetite and a smile. I can't take my eyes off the expression of genuine pleasure, as if the outside world didn't exist at all, as if he wasn't who he is and I wasn't who I am. He really must be a gullible idiot who never faced consequences based on his circumstances. But he sure is a handsome one, with an inviting mouth and a warm grin.

"You manage to suspend the existence of the outside world... And I'm at disbelief at how easy you do so."

"What do you mean?"

"You enjoy the domestic moments as if they are yours without question."

"Well... They are."

Do I need to explain to him how it is from my end so he could appreciate the difference? Is there a point? Why would I bother? Why not let Mo enjoy his innocence while it lasts, and have some fond memories for less blissful days? Maybe if I had had such a phase, I would have acted like him as well. I would have indulged in the present like a glutton. Maybe I would be a different person too.

"Tell me... What do you want to say?"

"I'm not going to bother explaining the sour to someone who has been reveling in different degrees of sweet. You will have to taste it to understand. So, for now, just enjoy it without the looming doom of the sour mouthful in the next bite."

"Fair enough... But why would you let the sour of the future bother you here..."

Mo points at his head.

"When right now all of this is just so sweet... So good."

"Fair point."

"Do you like the pasta?"

"I've had better."

"You're not serious? Better than this one? It can't be. I can't imagine!"

"When you've grown up in New York, good pizza, pasta and great food are your consolation prize. It's part of the deal."

"Maybe we could try your favorite place then?"

"I'm afraid they will serve us a side of knuckles with the best pasta in Brooklyn..."

"Ah... Screw pasta. How about pizza? Or the Chinese noodles?"

I can't resist his enthusiasm for food. I smile and nod, unsure what I am agreeing to. He must know we can't just go in public like ourselves everywhere. I'm not comfortable being out in the open with a man who is not a person of affairs, and reads closeted gay to anyone with a clue. I don't know whether he would be either. There is always this space right here, though, where he could nurture the illusion.

After some time in the bathroom, I come out prepared and he is at bed reading again. I slide against his chest and can't stop a gentleness from taking over. Luckily, Mo doesn't notice. He too has been too thirsty. He still doesn't allow room for anticipation, doesn't appreciate the buildup. He doesn't let me initiate and quickly takes over. I wouldn't have liked it, but I don't have the will to dexterously turn it around.

"Finally... Josef, I missed you... I missed this... I missed this a lot..."

I don't want him to talk, so I shut his mouth with my lips. We spend a feverish night where I let him lead, finding ecstasy in every turn. He couldn't do anything wrong at this point. He starts putting pressure in his fingers, and I'm keenly aware of their presence against me. There is nothing more I want than to have them for myself. I keep him close and bury my nose where I can't question the existence of anything beyond him.

Later, much later, I wake up to the smell of coffee and the noises at the kitchen. I look down and Mo shows me big croissant sandwiches.

"I got us food."

"What time is it?"

"Summer... Do you want some coffee?"

I caress my head and realize the hair is growing. I haven't shaved it in sometime. The thought that Mo's hands have touched it is embarrassing. How did I over-look my personal hygiene? It stirs melancholy within me. I don't want Mo to suffer my moods, but then I remember that my moods are shielded by my attitude. I remember the night of thrust and sublimation and my worries pale. I take care of myself in the bathroom, quickly shave my head with dexterity and have a small cut. I clean up and head downstairs. Mo is waiting for me by the table on his stool. His smile warms and wounds my heart at the same time. I don't know if I can keep this act for long. I acknowledged I was in a dangerous situation before. Now I'm no longer sure whether I gave up momentarily, or I'm still within a hesitant space. I come next to him. He kisses me and asks:

"Are you this cold and quiet when you wake up?"

"I don't usually have sleepovers."

"You don't have anything to be concerned about..."

"Hm... Tell me then. Have you had your fill yet?"

He answers with an odd certainty that brings up a side of him I haven't seen yet.

"No, not yet..."

"You don't strike me as a temperamental man. What would it take, Mo..."

"I have no idea so far myself... But if it's still all the same to you, then please give me at least the time to figure it out. You still don't mind, do you..."

The bastard. He can't suspect. He can't know. But if he can guess it? What a fucking bastard. He must just make wild connections between my inner life and my sexual performance. He has nothing else to work with anyway.

"As long as you don't require my commitment, all of my time, my attention, specific types of involvement and let's see, shall I give you a list?"

"No, all I'm asking is to give me some time. You make it seem so easy, but it's not the case for everyone. I don't know how you got such cold blood in you, but... Well, I'm starting to understand why it could be a perk in this place."

He eats while shaking his head. I glance at him and wonder whether approaching a relationship in such a way works. No, it's irresponsible to say the least. All Mo is thinking about, all he is preparing for is the point ahead where he will no longer find excitement or pleasure, where the pseudo-routine would settle, and he would finally be at leisure to dismiss me altogether. Maybe it will be a good deal by then. But for now, the scorpion key is not a good one. This is why I don't accept any sort of key: The respect inherent to having such an agreement is beyond the thrills and moods. It's reliable and trustworthy sustenance without the mercurial idiocies of a youth looking for sensations to feel alive. I know that because I have been through this cavalcade. As usual, I think of my peers and remember why they wouldn't deal with the virginal specie. When it all ends, what is left will be me, and how dependent or trusting in that illusion I would have become.

I clean the dishes more out of consideration than domestic life, then get to my Moog and resume my craft. I avoid taking a break lest the tension in the air would collapse. My instrument keeps me busy enough. The tracks remind me of the endgame, and the conditions aligning for it to be the optimal build for my music. I remember how ideal of a setting this is, how there is not just anguish and uncertainty and inner turmoil to it. The darkness is merciful too. I wouldn't think of hiding New York buildings out of my sight, especially if I made it far and well enough that I could afford to live on such elevated attitudes, in such buildings, at such a neighborhood. But I find something private and charming to this veiling darkness.

I don't go outside today and keep to my work, empowered by my significant progress and the perspective that I would be done soon. I would have the music I worked for fill up every mental space in other people's heads.

Then, I could disappear and forsake the Love Alcove for the rest of my life. But I have to play my cards right for that. Birthing the music is the start of the struggle, and quite paradoxically, the easiest part. Fortunately, I have figured out the rest of the steps, worked towards planting the seeds, established the required clusters to make efficient progress.

Evening is on us. I grab a glass of water and weigh my options: I could keep creating my music and have a fresh night inside. Or I could go outside to break the chance of any habit. I could take a long humid walk to think, or head to a hot discotheque to spend my stamina other ways. I could come back exhausted and avoid interaction. There are no feelings to spare in this relationship. Sooner or later, Mo will wake up to the world as it is and he will understand, in time, why things are the way they are right now.

"Josef..."

"Hm...?"

"You look good... If you made up your mind about it, can we fuck tonight?"

"You sure get excited easily."

"I can't help it..."

I head towards Mo. There is something seductive about his silhouette being straight over the large drafting table. I don't want to lock eyes with him yet. I stare at his drawing and discover entablatures with a detailed cross-section, further magnified to make up the patterns. The small notebook is open and secured to the top left of the table. He is reproducing the sketches on larger scale.

"Is that all you need to do with your days? Scaling up drawings?"

"It's not the exact design. I draft the basic idea in here and develop it later on the table..."

"And I'm assuming bars are a good place to find inspiration?"

"Yes, but no... They are good to evaluate how people mindlessly interact with the environment when out of control and without a care in the world. You'd think a bar would be a den of mistakes and accidents, but it's uncommon... There is something the design of these places capture that I have yet to put my finger on..."

"Why would you have such an interest in safety elements of design? ... The way I see it, architects design the building as a whole and care about the exterior, the elevated roof, the walls... The grandiose details that are unattainable to the general public, the decadence of a patio, the elaborate facades, the choice of rooms' alignment... All the elements which make a building a work of art have nothing to do with humans' daily motion."

"Well, you weren't listening... So, I understand... But I favor brutalist architecture. And it happens to be more than just outer design. It's a vehicle to the lifestyle and the economy of the community. It's a thought-up plan for living quarters and accommodations in the spirit of efficiency and productivity. I love that the most about it. It's not art for the sake of it. I don't believe art is meant to be useless motion captured for the sake of sheer entertainment. I believe art, or at least its ruling principle, is the respect of the motion and the current of life. Whatever man makes should abide by such a principle so that the efficiency and benefits of the created object are achieved in harmony with the standards of the times."

I smile, though secretly wounded by the explanation. It shouldn't. Mo is vacillating between being a craftsman and an artist. It's expected on a path like his own. All I needed was the confirmation he was more on the pragmatic side than the artistic one. Boxing art in such a narrow way is enough to pass that verdict.

"I know you must think in a radical way given your taste in music, and I respect that..."

"Thanks."

"But I will never understand what could possibly be appealing about synthetic melodies. They feel so industrial I'm surprised machines noises and traffic honking aren't part of it."

"I happen to have some of that too... A track that speaks of the Wicked City."

"Only in New York would that pass for music..."

I smile but tease him.

"You must expect a lot from your music."

"I must confess, Josef... I'm not much of a music person."

I'm not surprised.

"I don't mind it in the adequate occasions: For celebrations, for dancing, for the sake of the poetry within, as a background to a mindless activity... But the sort of music where you go to a concert hall and sit for two hours? That's something very Western and foreign to me. I don't think I would have the patience to sit through fifteen minutes."

"I see. Let's agree to disagree then."

"Are you going out?"

No, I no longer need to go out. Mo spoke enough to help cool the fury underneath my skin. I inhale the revelations, summon the poise and I am back to my assured and controlled persona. I take Mo on his couch. I am fully asserting my dance and myself in the action. It has been a while since I had a sense of my coordination and my movements. Mo tries to keep up, but he must have forgotten the dance where it's in-control me who leads. I am not about to cut him any slack. It's been a while since he dealt with the unbridled and carefree lust of a versed and methodical hunter.

Hand Whispers

If it weren't for the hotel's lobby, the occasional gigs and my Sunday walks in Central Park, I wouldn't have perceived the passing of time. The dark living room hides it well. Alternating between playing my instrument and fucking Mo has been a surreal experience. When I go outside, I have trouble placing myself back into the map of the real world. I need the rough rides of the bus and the subway to recollect, to find a way back to my usual composure. I even wished the gray mush of the hotel performances would grant me a better footing in reality. Somehow however, they have become easier to bear, and not as effectively painful as before. I was about to tell the hotel manager that I was ready to commit to more nights. I hate to admit it, but the domesticated dream has been an unpredictable source of sustenance.

Mo takes care of the food and the laundry. He doesn't ask me where I go when I leave, and he is happy to see me back when I step inside. He accommodates the music he doesn't understand, and doesn't disturb my boisterous examinations of the melodies that come to me. I ask him after intercourse, whether he had his fill. He is sure he didn't. I wonder, but I don't speak any further. Eighteen days into our curious ménage à deux, Mo asks:

"Josef, if you have nothing planned... We could go together to the Lunar nightclub. It's safe, it's good atmosphere."

I shouldn't be surprised he knows the place. Most fresh off the boat gays end up at the same spots. I am, however, surprised by the extent of the request. I assess him, expecting further explanation. But he waits for my answer.

"You will have to tell me how we jumped to going out dancing together."

"I've been trying to finish these things, and they're not about to be done. I want to unwind and thought maybe you'd want to come with me."

"You can go. No one is holding you hostage..."

"It's not that."

"I could also leave for the night if you need the apartment for yourself..."

He scowls, then seems to remember our situation, and states:

"We're both adults here. If this was the case, I would have told you."

"I don't mind this domestic routine inside a confined environment. But I'm not taking the fantasy outside."

"It's just dancing... And... Other homosexuals are there."

I suppress a smirk at his awkward wording and reply:

"You don't know who is watching. Everyone goes to these clubs, and I don't feel like justifying my presence with someone to every acquaintance I meet."

"But..."

"Mo, I'm telling you: If you want to go, go and have fun. Live up your youth, dance to your heart's content, fuck someone new, just be careful. I have been through all of this before. Once is enough for me. I'm over it."

He eventually goes quiet and nods. He leaves and seems unhappy about it. I scoff at such topics of bickering. I should have known: Giving a finger will result in asking for an arm, then a shoulder and it wouldn't stop.

It will be over soon.

I keep telling myself that, as my mind goes between staying with the Moog or going outside. I even have a mind of going downstairs and speaking with Fred, the doorman. We came to be on friendly terms: The middle-aged man thinks a sophisticated 'whitey' like myself who is humble and speaks to him like an equal is 'something else'. He is discrete and minds his own business, which is solid coinage. Mo pays him well. Sometimes, we both take the subway together while heading downtown. Mo is jealous of the connection.

"I don't know what it is, but I'm just a cash cow to these people. All I have for anyone in the New York service industry is a fist of money."

"Then, you're not a desperate case. Usually, it's either money or a knuckle."

"But he doesn't look me in the eye. He doesn't talk to me about normal things, except the weather."

"I'm not surprised. You move outside like you are running away from your surroundings. It won't put people at ease to talk, lest of all hardened New Yorkers."

"What does that have to do with it?"

"A person's character is first brought to life in the eyes of the other through their interaction with their environment. That is the least to have as a first assessment, before even getting to the part where a person interacts with another living creature. You escape interactions in your stares, your stride, and the way you move your arms and incline your head. Anybody who can read a room and has no concrete benefits to get from you will just avoid you, or dismiss you altogether."

"I guess you're right..."

"Then comes the part where you interact with others: Your ease with the activity, your ability to shoulder the risk or take the initiative, the full awareness while controlling the conversation, or letting it go to someone else... There is much to the exercise and it requires practice."

"I never had to practice such things before, though..."

"Before as in a bubbled sphere where you either interacted with those deemed 'inferior' to you who would butter you up, or those you deemed 'above' you who you will butter up?"

"I ... Yes, but... Yes. Well, yes..."

"You need to go outside a little and interact with life. On equal and risky terms. Then, you will find out there is much to learn and practice. The experience is invaluable."

He quietly stares at me, trying to speak then repressing it. All he does is take my hands and bring them closer to his face, kiss them with an earnest sincerity that is bittersweet. I am uncomfortable. He whispers to them.

"What are you saying?"

"Nothings... Just nothings... Maybe in another life Josef, maybe if we were other people, or met in different circumstances.... Maybe then, it wouldn't be nothings. But right now, it's nothings."

I understand what he means, and I don't reply. There is nothing else to add indeed. My tracks will soon be ready. All that is left is to have enough money to book the studio for as long as needed.

Mo sees me grab my Moog, and he asks in a panicked tone.

"Is it some gig? I can give you a ride."

"I will need it somewhere else. You don't have to."

I can't help myself when I add, reassuringly:

"I will be back..."

The thing is I'm not sure when I will be back. As long as the audio engineering is taking place, all my capacities are solicited, and I can lose the notion of time and of the yearning in my flesh. By the time I am done, however, will the fatigue be overwhelming enough that I could head straight to my bunk bed and sleep? Or will my feet take me back to the dark apartment? I play with the idea of spending the night at the studio. I could always change and take showers at the tacky hotel before work, and I have canceled all my other commitments for the two weeks studio recording will require.

Somewhere within, a part of me is grimly satisfied by this arrangement, and looks forward to the end of the reckless madness. A voice cajoles me into going back to the apartment to rest. It's a weak one, though, because truth isn't its forte; it doesn't want rest, it wants much more. The fact that I would come to lie to myself is a serious threat on its own.

I decide to take it one day at a time. I will see how my studio sessions go: If the distance is straining my performance, I will go back to the dark apartment and ride this wave for as long as I can. Otherwise, I will have to assimilate, once and for all, that this situation is different. Things are not the same as the past. Mo is not the same than that blasphemous figure. This is not the same. And it will be a long and painful process, and I'm not sure it will even be worth it. I don't know what else to do anymore.

I start early at Greenwich Village. Coffee is free and fresh at the studio, as long as I grab it when Otish is done brewing it. I get to work without delay and spend the day engineering the sounds I have been putting together, mixing, layering instruments and tracks and playing with the nuances of filtered sounds. This is why I share an apartment with five people and skip meals. This is why I prostitute my talent and spend my daylight owning up to the straight-man image. I don't tutor out of the joy of teaching. I don't bend and swallow for the sake of people's company. If it weren't for the fancy suits, for the reliable quality in providing what is familiar and amiable, for the trustworthy face and all the rest, I wouldn't even have access to this unique studio. The sound quality is specifically tailored and heightened for synthetic music. The available options and add-ons are smart, sharp and bring an alienating effect to the layering.

Mama could have patented this wealth of technology, and made a fortune out of it. Instead, all she wants is peace and space, a solitude well-earned, and the opportunity to find her way back to her art, to live her life as she wants to. Meeting this artist had proved to me the dream can become reality. It had allowed me to articulate my yearning and my goals into words. More than meeting a radical performer who made something out of nothing for herself, she provided me with concrete proof that it gets better. With money, it gets infinitely more possible. I'm no longer ill fitted to this world. I can carve a part of it for myself and fit it to my needs.

By the end of the day, I leave early for the tacky lobby hotel. I take a quick shower and change into a tuxedo I keep there for emergencies. The clothes are getting loose on me, so I keep a layer underneath to properly render the silhouette they were meant to drape. The evening is long compared to the day. I wish I could be at the studio and keep working on my albums. By the time I build momentum and get in the zone, I have to give it up for the necessities of life, wages for shelter and equipment. I eat plenty of peanuts before the performance and scan my audience. I think they are in the mood for whimsy and wonder. I delight them with a rendition of compositions from L'enfant et Les Sortileges. The night follows its course, and the requests and bills pile up. The lobby becomes an improvised swing scene. I push the dancing agenda with some dynamic play. The people sitting have to stand. The drunk ones are already dancing. The staff moves the furniture to improvise a dancefloor, and the liquor is shouted to the bartender.

While the elation is supreme, I try to keep all my focus on my crowd and dismiss the frustration building up within. I could be at the studio mixing, or at Mo's bed, or Mo's living room, or by Mo's side. I could be making music while he makes dinner or sketches buildings. I could be holding his hand in public or dancing with him in a discotheque. We could be strolling the park together at ease. We could kiss in public. We could speak of here and there and our past. This relationship is not future-proofed.

Stop it. Stop it. Stop it.

I make an abrupt stop to the music. People look at me stunned. I manufacture a wide smile and start escalating the sounds again in a flirty manner. Where would I be without the self-preserving reflexes? The energy comes back, more intense. No one suspects the lack of control, the anguish, and the inner turmoil. What could I possibly do? I have many glasses by my tip table at that point. Drink.

I reach out to the glasses and start drinking.

Drink, you bastard. Drink.

I invite someone to join me, give them directions to play two notes while I provide the rest. Anything to keep the focus outside. The requests are getting wild and I pour myself into making sense and progressive transitions between them, hitting the few notes that would matter to such ears. You want butchered music you hear in the elevator? I am your man. You want a drinking song? I will reprise a mourning one into a jolly shot suite for your sake. Ask away.

When it's past two, Luke is beyond happy. The place is becoming its own scene thanks to my presence. I know. You don't have to tell me, I was there. I saw the conditions. I worked them out. I built the momentum and I maintained it. I let him explain to me though, nod at his impressions and his two cents on my performance. Then I ask him to sleep in the hotel until the morning. Behind the bar counter would do, at the coat closet, by any part of the hidden floor, I don't care. He is surprised but accommodates me with a basic room.

The morning comes. I grab breakfast at the tacky hotel, then head back to the studio. The grim thoughts which have been swarming my head progressively disappear as I get back in the groove of my craft. I don't stop until Otish inquires about my schedule. I ask to spend the night here. It's a long shot, but I land it. I continue for a while until I can't feel my fingers anymore. I stare at them, and they remind me of Mo's fingers. I chase the memory of their pressure on my ribs and back. I give up and sleep.

For a week, I alternate between the tacky hotel and the studio. I push the audacity of spending the night at the studio for few times at this point. I know it won't fly well with the manager and he will put his foot the moment Otish mentions it in a passing conversation. At the hotel shift, I assess my options for the following night: Do I run the risk of being kicked out late from the studio without having any backup plans? Do I call it a night at a reasonable hour and let my feet guide me? Lady Mama has been gracious with her space so far, but I know better than anyone the artist shouldn't be in charge of their domestic aspects. I myself am surprised they let me push it that long. I suspect Mama has had her word on the matter. I'm not sure whether she likes me, or is curious about what I will end up creating. The few times when she was with me at the studio, we didn't speak much. She would have few questions about the acoustic choices I made or the origin of a sampling. Then, she would stay quiet, her figure still and her stare vague like that of a blind person.

I'm close to finishing. Only the polishing touches and I will be ready to let her hear my work. I suspect if she likes it enough, she could grant me that magical push with the label companies. I prefer not to think about the alternative; I can't imagine her disliking my art. Besides, I am also aware if she didn't believe I had some talent, if she hadn't liked my samples, she wouldn't have let me anywhere near her precious equipment. I know Mama will give me plenty of feedback, and I shall do my best to incorporate it. But I trust there are few tracks which will definitely make the cut.

Have You Had Your Fill

Thinking of Mo wanes when I'm at the studio. His existence becomes a bittersweet melody in the back of my mind, rather than the never-ending stream of memories of the present that has been, and the future that could never be. At times, the sensations become so visceral that they freeze me in an exhale, and I actively have to breathe air into my lungs. The music acts up as well, and I often notice it too late. My reflexes have to come forth more often than not. I tell myself the madness will eventually die. It has to, it usually does. Or does it ever happen? I don't remember letting things get out of hand, or for matters to take this long to settle into a pleasant camaraderie, a radical absence, or a mature transactional relationship. Time and environment are abrasive enough that they will make anything decay, including memories and carnal desires. I just need to wait for them to exercise their might. I have to summon new levels of patience, that is all.

"Peppa... Peppa..."

It takes me a second to associate with the name. They have been motioning at my direction for some time but I was absent-minded. One of the waitresses is already by my side. I barely have time to recollect, and center myself at the tacky lobby hotel. She swiftly whispers.

"Luke wants you to play something oriental."

I react from reflex, and initiate a fall into Scheherazade pieces. It must be some white dress wearing Middle Easterners again. Surely enough, the sounds of their conversation and laughter precedes them. The bunch usually happens to be exceptionally loud, but they are amongst the most jovial tourists and generous tippers. The staff is energetic and pampering them in every possible way. It will be an easy night: These guys don't care for the ambience or the music. It's all about the decorum of being in New York City. I smile at them and recognize the face of Mo after a moment. I've never seen him with an Agal or in a white dress before. His beard is trimmed, and that musk aroma I know too well pervades the air. He barely stares at my end of the lobby, and instead sits with his group close by. Old men and few youngsters are assembled in what seems to be an unofficial meeting. I control my breathing and my play. Luckily, I know the piece and let it effortlessly flow through my fingers.

Both hotel shift managers join them, as well as the owner and his secretary. Their presence disrupts the light atmosphere of the lobby, alienates the rest of the guests. None of the staff cares enough though. It's a matter of money, and no one is about to ask the white dresses to lower their voices, not smoke or not order food in the area. I don't know how I feel about the whole scene, but I'm sure this is not a coincidence. What does it matter anyway? There is nothing to worry about. Still, tightness is in my gut. I can't discern the exact reason.

The guests order drinks. Mo turns towards me with intent, then examines the scene around the piano. I hold his gaze and politely smile. He politely smiles back, then answers one of the old men's questions. I can't make up the discussion with all the cross-talking happening. Eventually, the waitress who serves them gets close to Mo, then leaves. She comes to me, and whispers while dropping a couple of Franklins in my fishbowl.

"They are asking for... For jazz. Something like Brooklyn... Or Harlem brand of jazz..."

I know what she is trying to say without saying. I nod with a confident smile. Inside, however, there is a looming dread. I start with a light repertoire and reprise few classics of the genre. I can get through this. It may get monotonous, but I'm not going to break it. Just keep it going. Add some refreshing takes. Let the music sink in the background, and let my piano and the piano player be forgotten and dismissed. Tonight, I'm not looking for the crowd to get acquainted with one another. I'm not getting to know the guests or building up an audience. Tonight, I just want to be done without losing control over my fingers, or getting into something I have absolutely no mind for.

Mo calls the waitress. But this time, the morning shift manager comes to me and says with a wide smile.

"Peppa... Do you mind playing something more dynamic? How about something Hampton-y or Duke Ellington-ish?"

I hide my discomfort at the uncanny requests, and instead smile and ask:

"That won't be an issue, Richard. I assumed the gentlemen would need background music more than a centerpiece..."

"Well, yes that too... Can you do both?"

"I'm on it."

He nods. The waitress drops more bills in my fishbowl. I increase the dynamic playing and focus on not letting the music come too alive, for the sake of the ambience and of my mental space. That bastard. That supreme idiot has no idea. I can't focus on the venue, can't piece words with faces or capture the atmosphere. I can't connect with the lobby while busy managing the music and my mind. Still, the drinks come, the cash fills up the fishbowl. The staff is standing by and eager to answer every whim. The anxiety is there. I can't fathom anything beyond it at this point.

Mo comes and throws few more bills. I barely stare at him, remember that he is a customer now, and breathe deeply before asking him with a smile:

"Any requests, sir?"

"Black jazz at its finest, please... Luke and Richard tell me you are quite the jazz pianist. Graduated with honors and whatnot..."

"Indeed. I'm afraid they extol my talent too much though."

He nods and says with an earnest expression.

"Well, let's find out tonight. I will keep them coming, just keep playing."

I nod with a smile while avoiding the pit of humiliation within. If he thinks this is a way to put me back in my place, I will show him. His group already asks him to join them back. They break for a lavish dinner. I struggle to keep the anger bottled up. At some point, my fingers start tingling. Old sensations threaten to take over.

I can't. I can't go back to that place with that monster. I can't. Mo, you fucking idiot, you fucking moron.

It's like Mo could spot the point where I am about to give up, and he sends the waitress to me. She looks at me worried and reiterates the clients' request with an anxious insistence, barely veiled. For a stupid moment, I think she worries about me, but no: Having a client repeatedly make the same dumb request is not good. It means the piano player isn't doing his job, and she doesn't know enough to discern whether that's true. All she registers is that it's a client, and they have good honest cash to spend, and we need them to spend as much as possible.

I want to take a break. I usually play for five hours straight but this time, I feel like I can't keep up with the performance without consequences. Yet, from the stares of the managers, this is the one night where such thing shouldn't happen. My mental space is threatened by the subtle toxicity.

Mo may be a petty youngster and an absolute bastard, but I can't fault him for this. He doesn't know. He has no idea and I can't reproach him anything. I can't make peace with that notion though, for the play has to stay dynamic and intricate.

He wants the complex pieces of an old repertoire I had buried, and I'm basically trying to open the gates of hell without waking the devil. But I can't make peace with that notion because my fingers are packing up the stress and becoming stiff.

So, I have to fight against my fingers too, for it's too late to get them back to a space of ease. But I can't make peace with that notion because the music in the lobby is resembling the music of my college years, and I'm an impressionable idiot who's direly paying for it in the practice room.

Why did I keep going back to that room? Why did I keep playing jazz? I already knew jazz wasn't for me. Why? Why? Why can't it be erased from my personal history once and for all?

"Peppa, play them something very Brooklyn. Put in some gusto. The gentlemen want to know the extent of your talent."

Richard enthusiastically shouts under the embarrassed and quiet demeanor of Luke. Luke would never speak to me this way, never raise his voice over the music or make such idiotic comments. But Luke is not the only one in charge, and right now, he's an employee as well, whose goal is to put the clients first, and provide them with the New York experience. I think I smile mechanically at this point. I'm not aware of it, but I'm already back there. I feel the cold piano cover against my chest. I muffle my pain with my fist. I want for it to end. Why did I go back? Why did I keep going back? It's not just him. It's every screwed conquest after that. It's the wild phase which could have cost me everything were it not for the wake-up call of his death. Why does the past not let go once and for all?

I still have some presence. I can whisper to myself.

This is not you, this is no longer you.

You learned and fast, you understood, you knew.

This won't be happening again.

This is no longer an option for you.

You've learned at every turn, you've internalized the lesson.

I hear my mother's voice in my head:

"It's okay Peppa, it's not the case anymore. I can do that now. We live in a free world."

I find myself whispering, my eyes blurry and my cheeks a little wet.

"It's not the case anymore. We live in a free world. It's okay... It's okay. We'll get through this too. We will, I promise. Just watch me."

At some point in the middle of my personal hell, Luke comes to talk to me. The guests are gone and it's time to close the piano bar.

"This was the best of you yet, Peppa! You were beyond words!"

I lift my hands and put my palms on my thighs. I shiver at the idea of moving my fingers.

"Anything for the customer."

"They are not just customers. They will be the new owners."

"..."

My lack of response and my neutral expression worry him. Luke has never seen me like this before.

"You must be exhausted, Peppa... You need some sleep, it will be busy days soon. They were shouting to the end of the corridor. We had guests complain. Oh well, it won't matter within weeks. The good news is they want to keep you."

I don't have the strength to ask. Luke carries on with an enthusiasm which belongs to another world than the one I exist in.

"After the renovations, of course. They will be re-opening, and they have been discussing all the details tonight. One can never be sure whether the new bosses would keep the employees. Good news for you: They love you, and want to promote you to head of the jazz band."

I don't even try to understand what he is saying. He sees my stoic face and asks:

"It's been a difficult night, I get it. Me too, man. I couldn't keep up with their discussions. They have way too much stamina for arguing, these Arabs. Do you want to spend the night here?"

I finally manage to answer:

"No. I will go. Thanks Luke."

"No Peppa, thank you! Everyone made a great buck tonight thanks to you."

I finally perform a smile, gather the money in the jar and leave. Once far from the hotel, I collapse by some stoops and hold my head. The evil inclination asks for malice, but I did radically cut ties with the self-destructive schemes. I breathe and breathe until all I focus on is my deep breathing. If I want a fighting chance, my breathing has to become all that exists in the now.

I don't know how long I'm by those stairs, but I breathe long and slow until my head is heavy and numb. I don't think twice and stop a cab. I give the address and am there within the hour. Fred greets me and I politely answer back.

I stare at the scorpion key and breathe. I put it in the lock, and it works. I come inside and Mo is there. He is having a drink by the kitchen counter, waiting for me. We stare at each other for a long moment. I don't know where to begin. I scowl at him as I close the door.

"Was that your idea of a sick joke?"

"No."

"A humiliation session maybe?"

"No."

"A bid for power?"

"Not at all."

I try my best to control my tone of voice and my words. He is an ignorant idiot, and I did well keeping him in the dark. But what he did isn't about to be dismissed. He doesn't realize the repercussions, and I don't want my own demons to inhabit somebody else's. It's incestuous and ugly. I've hated every second being on the receiving end. Now more than ever though, I can understand how it's so easy to just perpetrate the cycle.

"Then walk me through it."

"I doubt I can do that... I couldn't do it when you've done it to me. I'm not sure I can explain it now either... But you are having a taste of your own medicine and you're the articulate one. So maybe you can put it in words for me?"

"What are you talking about?"

"Exactly..."

He comes closer and stares at me, his hands in his shorts. He looks like himself, but his kindness and warmth were no longer there. I try to make sense of what is going on.

"We agreed on these boundaries. I thought we were adults. Whether I want to come back and when is not up to you."

"That's not it."

"So, you are telling me this whole night was not because I keep my distance from you as we agreed?"

"No, no, no..."

I see he is getting angry that I don't know. Before I can speak, he says with almost poison out of his lips.

"If you had kept it at this, I would have borne the pain. For you Josef, I would have made it work, one way or another. I came here to be free. To live life on my terms. Then you come at me, you treat me like a human being, like I was never treated before. You see my soul. You take me high. Then you let me fall in the ugliest way. You rob me of it all in the most disgusting way... You bring that fucking... You bring him and make me choose. You impose him and you make me feel like I'm just one of many, and I have to fuck myself, and that is all I will ever be; the closeted Arab Muslim from the Middle-East!"

I start understanding as he is unleashing his anger. Many things are mercilessly lining up in my head. Many things make sense under the light of his anger. I can't focus on them for his voice is too loud and stabbing.

"Don't read into it Josef, or should I say... Peppa... It's just jazz. Classic, jazz, the garbage you play... It's all the same to me. I just happened to be in the mood for jazz. After all, what would a college whitey of New York be possibly playing right now? Your folks are the usual buffoons of the new royal courts. And the royal court wants jazz, so you will play it for me for as long as I pay you... Ah! And don't read too much into it!"

I don't want to think anymore, but my mind is ruthless and methodic.

There is your reason, Josef.

Infatuation doesn't make a man spend nights outside and be relentless about his goals. It's sheer hatred. No... There is no love, so there could be no hatred. This is sheer malice. I have trouble recognizing the gentle and generous person in this vicious snake.

I want to ask if all that time, he was just waiting for his opportunity to bite, but I won't give him the satisfaction. He has no control over his emotions, and I am in possession of mine, so far. This fact brings my breathing to a deeper place as I face him and calmly ask.

"How did you know where I work?"

"The doorman helped me."

"The doorman helped you."

"You already know your people and your city, Peppa...
"

I hate when he uses my pet name.

"You Americans would do anything for money."

"So, you manage to bring your rich folks to a lobby to make a pianist play jazz?"

"That's all you are thinking about right now? The logistics?"

"Humor me, I'm curious..."

He is getting angrier. Maybe it wasn't how it would play in his head. At least I'm not giving him that.

"We are looking to invest in hotels. It's not hard to find places to buy for that. This whole street will become hotels or office buildings. To have another hotel downtown wouldn't disrupt my father's plans."

I nod. Truly. I bring the key to the table and he grabs my hand and asks, almost aggressively.

"You've got nothing to say for yourself?"

"What would you have me say? 'Well-played Mo'? 'You are learning now, Mo'? 'I told you Mo'?"

"God, you really are a coldblooded son of a cunt."

I throw a punch at him with my other hand and he retaliates. He throws himself with a wild aggression, and I easily secure him in a lock and add some punches. The rich boy doesn't know how to fight, and is letting his anger guide him. I could control him and leave it at that. I already have him after all. I could be above the insult to my mother. I could prevent the violent stream of my youth from pouring into him.

But no. I choose to beat the shit out of Mo throughout the apartment. I shove him on his tables despite his screams. I make sure to stamp on every goddamn building Mo didn't already crush. I only stop when he yells like a wounded animal and rounds his back to protect his last pieces.

I stop and look at the carnage. All the mockups were flattened and dispersed. His drafting table is on the ground, broken. I unsuccessfully try to even my breath. He holds something on his hand, and I hear the faint moans. I wonder whether I hurt him badly and I can't move. We gradually calm down until he sits and examines the Folie. I mutter despite my best efforts to be quiet.

"I hope you had your fill now..."

He cradles his useless building and whispers:

"I've had it tonight... When you couldn't fucking keep your tears from falling. When I could see someone hurt you fucking good. That, on its own, will bring me all the satisfaction I could never have had from fucking you."

"You're fucking poison."

"And you're a coldblooded monster."

I wipe my nose, and try to find some silence and calm after his bullets. I can't beat him again. I can't, not while he is not fighting back, not while he's sitting like that. He looks so broken and meek.

"I was never a coldblooded one. But thanks to you, I'm learning..."

I push against my nose until the bleeding stops. He doesn't turn, he doesn't stand up. We are quiet for some time. I could let my anger and pain pour out, or I could leave and internalize everything, mostly how much of a fucking idiot I have been. I doubt any measure of intelligence would have prepared me for this experience, though.

"Thanks for the money. I can afford not to see your fucking face anymore."

I leave before Mo finds any words, that is if he has any to start with. I walk New York City's streets until I can't walk anymore. I get inside a bodega, grab a cheap meal and a dirty coffee. I sit in a corner in front of the window, and finally let the events of the night catch up with me. I hold my eyes in my palms and hide my tears, muffle my cry. It was too vicious. He is the poison, and he was the remedy. My mother tells me to stop crying, that we are free now, that this is the life of freedom and we can hold hands now. She tells me this is America, this is freedom and gullible me believes her. Gullible fucking me thinks my mother's freedom is mine as well.

Mama

Comes daylight, my soul is a pile of shattered pieces, but my tears have dried and my mind has settled. The insistence of the sunshine puts me into my routine. I head back to the Greenwich studio and take care of the technicalities. I'm not there in the process, but my hands already know what needs to be done. I wrap up earlier than the usual and head to my rental. My roommates aren't surprised at my erratic appearance. They notify me of the upcoming performance dates and practice. I collapse in my bed and give into disturbed sleep. The viciousness of the previous night echoes once in a while, driving the poison deeper, and all I can do is internalize the pain and sit with it, wait patiently for time to let me move on, and to let the lesson settle. Distress and regrets fight over whatever is left of the shattered pieces of my soul.

I told you so, I knew it would happen.

Listen better next time.

If you need to actively alienate someone, just leave.

You will find someone else who doesn't care at all, who is equally twisted, and you will be a good fit for each other.

Why bother setting boundaries with those who don't understand them?

Do you understand now?

If they don't speak the language, don't bother.

You thought you were cleverer than your peers when you were stupider.

Enjoy the aftermath, Josef.

I resume my work at the studio despite the horrible night. I'm almost done. Besides, nursing a broken soul in stillness and tears is not my style. That at least, I still preserve. An anxious question rises while I take a bathroom break: Do I go back to the tacky lobby hotel? What if he goes there? I had actively avoided thinking about his name or his face since that awful night, and I find the hint of a mental image hurtful enough. I struggle to not fall into a miasmic mood, and wonder how stoic I would be. Would he have the guts to show up? Or more poison in him to diffuse?

Coldblooded monster... I remember all his work crushed on the floor. All his time and discipline wasted within seconds. I didn't do this out of cold blood. If anything, my blood runs warm, and it was on fire. Because of him. I tried my best to navigate something tricky without compromising anything. But in the end, I'm the coldblooded one. Maybe it's true somewhere. I thought about my actions before throwing him against his precious buildings. It could have been me thrown against my instrument, my labor of years destroyed within seconds. The thought of it makes me shiver. But I have no empathy for him at the moment. I don't know what I wanted to do: Hurt him as much as he hurt me, get back at him for viciously violating my sole sacred space, or bring an end to the bastardization of everything I held for an acquired territory, and valid virtue.

While I'm collecting myself in the bathroom, Mama comes inside.

"Peppa...?"

"I'm here, Milady..."

She has a faint smile. I know she thinks it's ridiculous, but I also know she likes being addressed in such terms.

I freshen up and come out to meet her. Her dogs are with her. She dismisses Otish, and energetically makes way to sit by the giant Moog unit. I clear my throat, become alert and lean by the counter while waiting.

"Let's hear it."

"I'm.... I'm not completely done yet. I am still sorting out the tracks..."

"Well, best time to hear it then. Let's sort them out together."

"I... of course... I didn't want to trouble you, Lady M."

"What I find troublesome is to not know what you are working on... I'm sick of being patient Peppa... Let's hear it."

I nod and line up the songs to play. She is impressed by the number of tracks I produced, and goes through them efficiently. Mama doesn't comment much, but takes liberties in making modifications, decreasing the tempo of few and adding some mixing of her own. I can't help but be at awe at her incredible acoustic sensitivity and her efficient modifications. She is able to zero in on auditive byproducts of interferences, and weed them out within few seconds, whereas I take a good twenty minutes. She is undeniably the master of the instruments and an exceptional artist.

"Peppa dear... I think I will need the dogs out for a second. Can you take them for a walk?"

I understand and nod.

"Thank you. They haven't pooped yet, so do you mind grabbing some bags on the way out?"

"Not at all, Milady..."

I leave her and take the five poodles on a stroll. The garden surrounding the house is neat and clean. I quickly finish the tour though while paying attention to the poodles, then decide to go outside for a longer walk. I let Otish know I will be back in an hour and we head to the suburban streets of the neighborhood.

The traffic is muffled and far away. The residents mind their business, walk their dogs, hop from the car door to the building door or vice versa. I recognize few and stop for small talk. The people who are walking to get somewhere are the help. I stare at the chic penthouses and the sophisticated little gardens, thinking of the day where I would live here as well, provided they don't turn into more hotels and offices. Or worse, folies straight out of Middle-Eastern visions. The thoughts make me sad, so I busy myself with the poodles. They are not receptive to my attempts. Just like their mama, they are old, stoic and over everything at this point. But they look good and have their own personal games with each other.

When we come back, I clean my hands and wait by the patio next to the garden. Few days ago, such a situation would have been a scary experience. Few days ago, I would have ached under the weight of the anticipation. But the melancholy has addled my sensations. I am calm and contemplative of the bees on the flowers, the sunshine on the fountain waters and the colorful birds stopping by the trees. Otish brings us drinks and sits next to me. I try to initiate a cheerful toast.

"Cheers to Mama... Her ladyship of moistened harmonics."

"Cheers to Mama... And to paying the bills."

"That too..."

"You've been a bit off lately. The music is playing a number on you?"

"No... Just people... It's exhausting to actively deal with people."

"We wouldn't know here... But I can imagine. I thought maybe it's some creative bottleneck..."

"No, thankfully... Creative output is the sane part of my life right now..."

"If Mama had that, everything else would fall into place..."

"No inspiration yet?"

"No indeed... And it's a sour topic... Whenever she decides to give it a try and it doesn't work, she just relapses. It's like... I think she thinks she lost it when she decided to fully move forward... With... Everything."

I know Otish won't push the notion. We both have but a vague understanding what lady Mama is going through, and can only trust her few words on it.

"I... it's messed up when the personal history clings on to the art and turns it into a rancid reminder."

"Something of this sort... I guess... But at least, she has you to keep the studio alive and challenge the equipment."

I scoff. What a sad bunch we are after all: An affluent genius pioneer with nothing more to share with the world, and the broke monster with too much to give but no outlet.

"And I think it keeps her engaged to hear what is on the streets and clubs of the city without going outside herself..."

"It's been years now..."

"It won't change..."

"What about you?"

"Man... I thought I will do this gig for a while, get enough money, peace out.... But now, I'm not sure I want to leave her alone like that, or with some inconsiderate jerk who's after her for her money."

"But what was of you? Before? You always wanted to be an assistant?"

"Not at all... I used to work for Mama to get the hang of the craft and open my own label someday. I have a degree in music but also music management and business, from Boston Conservatory..."

"What is that?"

We discuss the programs of the university, and what it has to offer in the new economy. It made sense that such a complicated practice would be taught in a structured manner, but I haven't known people in that line of work with degrees. Still, I like the appeal of the niche field and the thought of concentrated experience taught in segments and classes. The assistant generously explains the details. I am thinking about it and I hear Mama call me.

"Good luck... I guess."

"Thanks."

I go inside at the same time than the dogs, and look at lady Mama's benevolent smile.

She doesn't waste any time and she mentions in her matter-of-fact tone:

"Thank you for waiting Peppa... I have to say I'm very, very pleased."

It doesn't register with me at first. She isn't someone who sugarcoats or smiles for the sake of it. Yet, she is staring at me and is smiling right now.

"You are... You liked the... The track that is..."

"I liked few the best, as in I want them played during my funeral, Peppa... But I loved all the works you've created. Thank you for letting me in on the experience."

I don't believe it. I was expecting her to like a few and praise one or two. I try to talk but the emotion is shocking me.

"Mama, you are not playing with me, you..."

"Not at all, Peppa... You're the playful one. I'm the old crone who can't spare a joke anymore. I physically can't at this point. My doctor says my stomach is weak."

I sit down and put my hands against my face, feeling the heat and the tears. I can't possibly cry. Come on, get it together.

"Mama... I don't know what to tell you... I didn't expect this response..."

"I took the liberty of shuffling the tracks' order and coming up with three albums. I think you have three albums worth of music here. You also have four themes, but we can lump two together. I also think you need to practice more how to clean layered sounds and filter natural ones. Overall, it's a journey. If you don't mind, I will have a rough duplicate and will compensate you."

"You don't need to compensate me, just make a copy... It's an honor Mama, it's always an honor with you..."

"You're too sweet. But I'm not done. I need to compensate you Peppa, because this will be the main listening delights I will get for some time, and because I doubt you will be able to get a record deal."

"Ah..."

"I can always get these to the moneybags, but I doubt they will give it enough credit to grant them due diligence. I don't know how precious these albums are to you...."

"Mama, they are everything...."

"Then, whatever label ends up picking them will not treat them accordingly."

"I'm not settling... Not for this... Not this time."

"Listen Peppa... You are a raw musician. A deeply sensitive creature... And a self-aware man. I can hear the epiphanies of your heartbeats and the salt of your sweat in these tracks. Some of them are intense enough that I live your pain and your warmth, and I am right now full of you in the inside. My soul recognizes the soul in you, do you understand?"

I nod.

"That's why I don't want you to sell your creation for cheap money. Don't compromise on it for the sake of an audience who needs to be spoon-fed. If you want that, make art which sells. Dimension it to appeal to labels and people who listen to the radio. But don't touch this one. Don't compromise it."

She finishes me off by adding with her vague yet ominous blue stare:

"I know the temptation is there. I know how hard it is outside in the streets, but don't pimp it up."

To think my concern was that Mama wouldn't like it. This is more violent than a simple difference of taste. Her expression is melancholic and understanding when she adds.

"I am where I am today because I have done it. In many ways. I'm grateful for what I have but look at me now. What's the point of having the setup and the big house in the Village when all my best tunes have been tampered with? Corrupted? Diluted? And where I had to break my work into pieces and transmit it in other ways? According to other... Whims?"

I struggle to tell Mama how wrong she is, mainly because she is stubbornly wrong, but also because all the counterarguments lie in a past and a dead persona who she doesn't want to associate with anymore. I understand the fact, but I find it hard if not disrespectful of her to dismiss her early works and how much it meant to many.

"But you paved the way. If it wasn't for you Mama..."

I sound absolutely ridiculous. How do I convey to this woman that I grew up listening to her music, that her works were the only possession my mother and her parents ever brought here, and that it was the drive to keep the hope and to inspire them to open discotheques and bring dance to the new world? How do I explain to her how much her art had mingled with my head growing up, and the countless evenings we spent dancing in the living room to her music?

"You severely underestimate how much you mean to a whole generation out there. I don't know what that was. but what you accomplished wasn't selling out."

She remains stoic through my emotional state, as I try to force something sensible out of my mouth.

"And yet, Peppa, you only heard the distorted version. You never listened to the original work."

"Whatever it was Mama, it didn't lose its substance. And that's what I want to offer as well... Mama, I don't need to tell you... You opened up a door of possibilities, a freedom in an otherwise rigid practice. You can't possibly believe it's nothing."

"Admittedly... But here I am today... I have nothing of my own. This self has nothing of her own. I shed so much skin to become my authentic self only for her to not be able to reproduce the miracles of the first age... I know what you mean Peppa, and I don't belittle that. I'm very grateful for it. It's what pays the bills, and keeps my seat on the table even though I no longer bring anything new to the table. But I can't stand remembering my old tracks, and I am incapable of making new ones. I thirst for something which would remotely feel like what I felt while making and listening to these early works, and I have been incapable of finding any so far... You have it in you Peppa, and you could do more with it on your own terms. It comes with consequences. But in the end of the day, it's art which yearned to be birthed and wasn't artificially made through and through for the sake of a market, of an audience and tailored according to certain demands."

She sighs and says, and I understand it's her attempt at sarcasm:

"We make electronic unnatural music. We are the freaks of nature. We know nothing of the organic miracles of sounds and life... Yet somehow, the other bunch are the people who make music based on demands, on commissions, on popularity, on the trends of the time, with a specific audience or marketing scheme in mind... Tell me Peppa, do mothers birth with such intentional dimensioning within their wombs? Because I'd like to have a word with mine if that's the case."

We both keep quiet. She finally asks.

"Do you think it normal art has become a commodity like anything else? That you have to take something so pure and right out of your soul and shape it into something else for the sake of some stranger who will whistle to it one time, dance to it in some disco, then remember it sporadically as a byproduct of a memory?"

I am defeated by that point. I struggle to answer.

"This is a difficult and complex question, Mama..."

"Only because you haven't been on both ends of it. I swam that sea. I crossed that bridge and I know you enough to know how much it will eat at you, should it happen to you."

"Maybe it won't... It's a new decade, there is chance they will like my work for what it is..."

"I encourage you to try. Maybe I'm senile at this point, out-of-touch with the public. Maybe this world is ready for you after all. I hope it's the case and I hope I'm wrong. But I tell you what: If we could go back in time and I was offered the choice to listen to this wizened me instead of the young me, I will pick the old one to listen to."

We are both quiet. I internalize her advice and nod. She proceeds to making copies then asks me:

"Peppa, what was happening between tracks 17 and 23?"

I am stoic for a moment. I can't repress the sadness seeping through. My face betrays me.

"It's... It's complicated Mama... My lust got the best of me."

"It didn't feel like lust to me."

I can't talk. Repressing my tears and pain is hard labor on its own. She glances at me and says:

"This is the part I don't miss about my youth. Don't worry Peppa, it will fade away quickly enough. All that could subsist would be food for your soul and your craft."

Finally, I stare at the ground, let few tears fall and ask with a rough voice:

"Are you sure?"

"Oh, Peppa..."

She comes closer to me, and kindly passes her hand around my bald head then hugs it against her chest.

"As certain of it as I am of my name...."

I smile through my tears and feel better. I don't know how she did it, but it is already less poignant.

"Finally, a smile... Akh... You would give me all the money in the world, and I wouldn't go back to this age."

"What if that is the price to finding a way back to your voice?"

She stops for a moment. I just hope I didn't offend her.

"I have to think about it later."

I leave the Greenwich studio with my equipment and few records. New wind is under my wings. Right now, New York City feels so big and of endless opportunities, just like the city I grew up in. I want to make the most out of this high. So, I drop by the hotel to resign for personal reasons. They try to convince me otherwise, then suggest a vacation. I thank them and leave. I play the gigs with my band at certain nights. I avoid the old venues and the Love Alcove. I avoid everyone and everything. I too walk like a thief in the streets and box my head within my body to radiate unfriendliness. I don't want to take any risks. I even find the cheapest studio in lower Manhattan where I move in with all my belongings. I prioritize good sleep and minimal disturbances. I focus on meeting with heads of music production, label companies, professional connections and all the circuits which I had set up all these years.

I had come up with a marketing plan and a document for the potential audience, radios, tracks to be released as singles or on the waves. I have different shades of feelings to share. Those who want upbeat will find what they are looking for. Those who ask me for ambience tracks get satisfying answers. I keep busy with these meetings, presentations, and run-through of my documents. Then I practice with the band. At night, I'm too exhausted to give into my dark thoughts, and disrupt the painful mending of my fragmented soul. The following morning, the dynamic routine resumes.

Every day, however, I am less hopeful. I get offered to work from scratch on a soundtrack or get referred to some underground club to perform. Some tentatively mention European disco scene. At several corners, what Mama predicted, what Mama feared, was waiting for me. And thanks to her voice of reason and the bittersweetness which had settled in my soul, the marathon to the promised life has stalled. I reconnect with my observational and analytic faculties. I see the compromises which hold no guarantee and no aesthetic. I can reason without the rush of making it, or the interfering desire to have three meals a day. Maybe the goal has to change after all: I can make my own music, I can mix it and produce it, but I can't distribute it yet. I can't make sure it reaches the people who would appreciate it for what it is. Maybe this is what I have to work on after all.

I meet my mother in Central Park and let her lead the conversation. I don't want to involve her with any of my processes, only the results. Right now, there is no concrete prospect, so I just give her the usual answers: Still working on tracks, tutoring, playing, performing with the band. Yes, I eat right, I just can't seem to put on weight. No, I'm too busy for a girlfriend. No, my roommates are single as well. We are all focused on our careers. The funny thing is that my mother seems to know I'm gay, but thinks it's something that will go away with time. A phase, a temporary fancy, or a consequence of living in America. She exclaims in Czech while in the middle of the conversation.

"Look at your scalp, Peppa... You cut your head again!"

"It's fine, it heals fast..."

"Ah! That is not good, not good at all. I should have asked someone how to take care of your hair."

"I like the buzz cut better. Hair is too much pampering. Look at you! You always spend too much time and money on your hair when you could be doing something else."

"Well, your father likes it when it's wavy and I happen to look good like that."

I scoff. She makes the same request as usual.

"I'm sure if you come for dinner, he will be very happy."

"Let that dragon sleep, mom. I have too much to handle right now. A fight with dad isn't ideal."

"You guys won't fight this time."

"You shouldn't be so sure."

She grabs my hand with intention, and gives it small slaps as if I were a child.

"What is wrong with you? Fighting your father? Do you want him to lose the rest of his teeth?"

She moans about my bad manners. I laugh and grab her hand, instantly comforted by the long, elegant palm firmly holding mine.

"Mom... I have been thinking... I may go back to university after all..."

"Oh, what for?"

"Like granddad..."

"Your grandparents didn't have a university degree..."

"I want to be in the music business..."

"Music business... Oh, sounds like there is money in that."

I nod. I feel something in my neck, but I refuse to answer it. Someone is staring at me, I'm sure of it. Let them stare. I'm not giving in anymore, I learn fast and I don't make the same mistakes twice.

I turn to my mother and say:

"I had a dream few days ago... A dream about a long time, when we were alone in the Brownsville apartment."

"Yes?"

"Remember when you showed me your picture with Dad."

"Yes..."

"And how you both were five feet from each other?"

"Ah... That picture? You should see the new pictures we have now."

"I cried when you showed me that picture... But I don't remember why."

"Son... It's..."

Her Czech is back again.

"Son, it's a sad story and I don't want to make you sad again."

"I was already sad. I just want to know why. It is irritating to not be able to remember, yet to feel the sadness all the same."

"Oh Peppa, that head of yours is impossible! You have to remember it was a different time. People like your father weren't allowed to do many things or be with people like me. I was fresh off the boat and stupid at that time. I see your father at the park almost every day, reading and I think Aaah, what a serious and mature young man. I walk in front of him in my best clothes, drenched in perfume and he doesn't even look! Oh! All the boys in the neighborhood look at me. All try to grab my tiny waist and invite me to dance. How come it's working on them but not on him? One day, I see him read Anna Akhmatova and I get so excited! I don't even think. I sit next to him, we talk the whole evening about her. I studied her in school before coming to America.

I like her very much. Your father was studying literature in university and reading her out of curiosity!"

"I remember his books, yes."

"I came to the park every day to talk to him. We walked together but he was scared somehow. I thought maybe I'm too exuberant to his taste. Ah what a waste, what a waste such a fine and smart and polite young man who reads poetry! One day, I can't resist and I make a scene and I hold his hand. We walk very happy. He tells me he loves me plenty plenty, and I tell him I love you so so much, like the Americans. But then, people come and they beat him up, shout at him and they don't let me come near him. I don't see him in the park anymore. I had to go to the university and pretend I was a student to see him. But even then, I was so scared they would hurt him again, so I would bring him books with letters inside to tell him that I still love him and I want to marry him."

"I remember that part... I didn't remember... The rest."

"Oh you cried so much Peppa... When I told you your father was badly hurt because I was stupid. It was a lot. I couldn't make you stop crying. I tried to make you feel better, but you asked for your dad, you asked if someone killed him outside. I didn't know what to answer. Your dad was abroad. I didn't know anything... I didn't..."

I hold my mother's shoulder and kiss her head.

"Sorry mom... Children are stupid."

"Yes, they are. But you aren't stupid anymore. Right, Peppa?"

I wholeheartedly laugh. This has been the first time I laughed in ages. It's the beginning of fall in New York. The trees are gorgeous and haven't lost their foliage yet. The day is long and the sun is warm. I kiss my mother affectionately and keep her close while I reassure her.

"Don't worry. Not only I'm no longer stupid, but I get sharper every day."

ρφ

In Memory of Doug Glaze

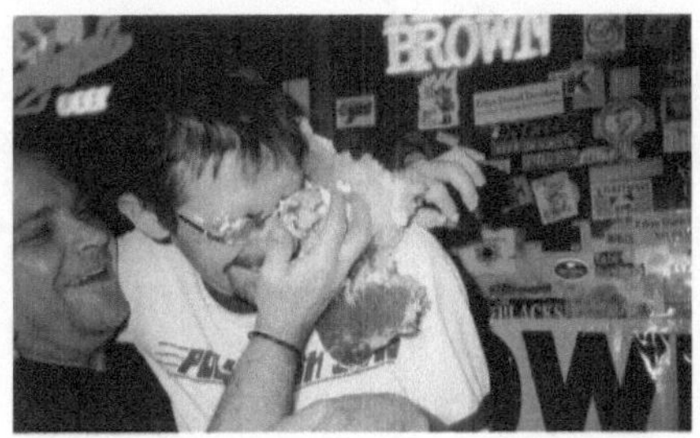

The AIDS pandemic has had an eerie and rancid impact on the conservative regions of the U.S. Many unsung heroes of little big towns, rural areas and abrasive communities have left a legacy that grows all the more impressive, as we witness firsthand, in this day and age, the passivity of a public resigned to fatalities, the absence of active assertive support to marginalized communities, and the glamorization and dulling of notions such as activism, rebellion and community engagement.

Doug Glaze from Kansas was a fierce fighter on the frontline of the AIDS pandemic during the 80s and 90s. He countered discriminatory laws, joined protests, gave presentations, reached out to black and rural communities to raise awareness, facilitate access to free testing and counseling for HIV patients and their families. Doug had been open about his HIV diagnosis, which he contracted when he was a teenager. He lived on his terms, and fiercely, to the end while serving the Wichita and Kansas community, more often than not uncredited.

For more information about Doug's legacy, visit: http://mmarlett.com/F5/news/index.php?pubdate=2003-03-06&story=339

Positive Directions has been the main NGO Doug served the community through. They still operate and welcome donations. All profits from this novella go to them. For more information, visit: https://www.positivedirectionsks.org/

Acknowledgments

Many thanks to those who helped our project transition
from private notes to a public platform.
Our deepest gratitude to Minimums for their ongoing
support, for Thomas, Tom, Nathaniel, Gail and others
for their priceless insight, and the encouragement of
several Clouds in the Aquarium.
Finally, thank you to the Kansans who introduced us to
Doug Glaze and his activism and legacy.

On Authorship

The Werths is a collective, operating under pen names. This helps us in the quest of consolidating our literary work separately and according to available means so that we can share them with a wider audience, while ensuring we keep our anonymous lives and free agency over being part of the world as it unfolds organically, and writing to our own rhythm.

The focus is therefore on the narratives, the characters and the tackled ideas. We don't cater to personal narratives and marketing the people behind the artist and have no social media presence save for the official website of the Hurry to the Capsule Atelier.

We thank you for your interest, appreciate your readership and hope you found something in our texts.

A Hurry to the Capsule book
v 1.0
www.hurrytothecapsule.com

Next: The Estuary in Boston

A restless Pepa is becoming increasingly sloppy while trying to establish himself in Boston's gay underground scene and launch his career in the music industry. His path collides with Mikuláš Vyvý, an untested Czechoslovak immigrant and formidable piano virtuoso. Their unlikely partnership offers promise, but frictions over assimilation, identity, and what it means to make art in America threaten their budding friendship.

The reader is advised the sexual passages are written in an explicit manner.